Arizona Payback

When an attempted bank robbery goes wrong, the outlaw gang led by Captain Parsons, an ex-Confederate officer, is forced to scatter. One of the men, Brad Mantle, finds a temporary job as foreman on a ranch owned by a beautiful Mexican girl. His fellow outlaw, Paul Shand, falls in love with the young girl who owns the bank the gang had raided.

Soon both men find themselves fighting to defend the girls' business interests from unscrupulous predators. But then the outlaws regroup and Parsons once again demands the loyalty of Mantle and Shand. Will the pair return to their old ways or are their new ties too strong to break?

With enemies coming at them from all sides they must seek new allies to help them if they are to survive the inevitable showdown.

Arizona Payback

ROBERT EYNON

A Black Horse Western

ROBERT HALE · LONDON

ISBN 0 7090 6977 4

Robert Hale Limited
Clerkenwell House
Clerkenwell Green
London EC1R 0HT

Typeset by
Derek Doyle & Associates, Liverpool.
Printed and bound in Great Britain by
Antony Rowe Limited, Wiltshire

Dedicated to
John and Anita, Arwel and Eirwen

ONE

Paul Shand's chestnut gelding seemed just as relieved as his rider to reach the brow of the long hill and see the hamlet of Twin Springs spread out below them. It was late afternoon and the July air was heavy and sticky as if the elements were gathering strength for a storm. Shand turned round for a moment and savoured the view of the New Mexico mountains which shimmered and swayed on the northern horizon.

It took almost half an hour to complete the descent to the plain, and the horse took advantage of the leisurely pace to slake its thirst in the pools of clear water left by the recent rains. Then they were in Twin Springs itself, a small township boasting a few shops, a single saloon, and bank and an adobe jailhouse whose door hung crookedly on its rusty iron hinges.

A handful of residents watched him ride past

them and dismount outside the saloon. They seemed lifeless in the summer heat and not even the expressions on their faces changed when he nodded in their direction. He was just another travelling cowboy, though unknown to them he was carrying a hundred dollars on his person, money he'd saved up over the previous year by depriving himself of many of the pleasures cowpokes notoriously indulged in. Although only twenty years of age, Shand was dreaming of a fresh start but if he'd been asked he couldn't honestly have said how he was going to use the stake he'd built up so carefully and laboriously.

He tethered the gelding to a post outside the saloon, mounted the steps with a stiff gait and pushed aside the swing-doors. The place was as quiet as he'd expected it to be; two smartly dressed businessmen were sitting in a corner of the room discussing their affairs in low, secretive tones, and four old-timers were playing cards at a table close to the bar. As the newcomer approached, the bartender, a slim, walnut-skinned fellow with eyes like a weasel, moved to meet him and ask him for his order.

'Make it a beer,' Shand told him. 'The colder the better.'

It tasted very good after a day on the trail. It was nice, too, just to stand there and watch the old-timers play and jaw, and feel the life come back slowly into the muscles of his legs. This wasn't a rich town; at least, the old fellers were playing for very small stakes and it was a friendly game. After a while, one of the players looked up from his cards and spoke to him.

'D'you play poker, young feller?' he enquired. 'You're welcome to join in if you like.'

'Hold on, Will,' another player joked. 'What if he's one of them professional gamblers from back East?'

Shand joined in the laughter. Well, why not, he thought, they were only playing for nickels and dimes. He went to get an empty chair from another table but suddenly the player with his back to the counter got to his feet.

'You can sit here, mister,' he said. 'My eyes ain't so good and they get tired so that I cain't see the picture cards too well.'

'Picture cards . . .' another old-timer remarked. 'When did you last get dealt a picture card? That's why you're chickening out, you quitter!'

It was all good-natured fun, and the man muttered something about having a home and a wife to go home to as he scooped up his money from the table.

'Well, you get a share in that for a start, young feller,' he said, pointing to the communal bottle of whiskey in the centre of the table. 'Don't let 'em do you out of that.'

Shand sat down and the next moment the bartender had come to the table bearing a clean glass in his hand. He picked up the bottle and filled the glass to the brim. Shand looked up at him.

'Like the gentleman said, it's paid for,' the bartender confirmed. 'All you got to find is your stake.'

The cowboy fished a handful of coins from his pocket and placed them on the table in front of him. One of the players pushed the pack of cards towards him.

'You deal, young feller,' he told him. 'That's stranger's privilege in this saloon.'

'Dammit, Alby,' another old-timer said. 'Let the man take a drink, won't you. We ain't got no place special to go, so what's the hurry?'

They were a pleasant little crowd, and they smiled and joked a lot. When the bottle was empty they called for another, then another, but there was no question of Shand paying for any of the whiskey. It seemed that that was another privilege strangers enjoyed in the township of Twin Springs.

As the game progressed the stakes rose slowly but steadily and the group became more animated. No one player at the table seemed to be doing unusually well, yet the newcomer had the uncomfortable feeling that the game was going against him. When he had a good hand he rarely made much gain from it, since the others invariably had hands too weak to bid with. When the stakes were raised he always seemed to come off second-best when he called. He guessed his luck was bound to change if he persisted. How much was he down – thirty dollars, forty. . . ? He drank some more whiskey and tried not to think about it.

For no particular reason his gaze came to rest on the free hand of the player opposite him. It was resting on the table, with four fingers extended and the thumb curled under the palm. Shand looked at his own cards. Was it a coincidence that it contained four eights? Shand attempted to bid on it, but the three other players all stacked their cards with their usual expressions of disgust at what fate had dealt them.

When the next hand was dealt Shand received no better than a pair of deuces. He glanced across the table and noted that his opposite number had withdrawn two of his fingers. This time all players showed an interest in bidding. Shand immediately stacked his hand.

'It's no good,' he sighed. 'I'd only be bluffing.'

He yawned loudly and turned in his seat as if he was searching for a wall clock that would tell him how late it was. Glancing upwards he saw that one of the bar mirrors was tilted forward, allowing him a clear view of the table. The man opposite him no doubt enjoyed the same view, including a clear sighting of the faces of the cards he was holding. Shand stood up suddenly and made an announcement.

'I guess I'm through for the night, gents,' he told them. 'Now, if you don't mind, I'll relieve you of all the money the three of you have chiselled me out of. If you don't like the sound of that, maybe I'll call the town marshal and let him settle matters.'

Something moved behind him and he swung round, drawing his Colt smoothly and swiftly. The bartender found himself staring into its barrel and he released his hold on the shotgun he kept behind the bar. It clattered noisily on to the floor and then all was silent again.

'Don't be stupid,' the cowboy warned them all. 'Money ain't worth dying for.'

He scooped up the banknotes and larger coins from the table. There was no time to count it or calculate what was coming to him. He backed his way towards the doors. The two businessmen were sitting just as frozen and still as the card-players but he didn't reholster the six-gun that was keeping him in charge of the situation.

He felt the woodwork of the swing-doors on his back and he pushed his way through them. He half turned and almost bumped into a huge bear of a man who was standing at the top of the steps of the sidewalk. Before Shand had time to react he felt a searing pain at the back of his head as the sky caved in on him.

He woke briefly but his head ached badly and his stomach was soured by the whiskey he'd consumed in the saloon. The early sunlight was strong enough to hurt his eyes and he closed them immediately. Somewhere nearby two men were arguing; it was about money and how much was owed by one to the other. In his present condition it made no sense to him, so he let himself slide back into a deep slumber.

It took vigorous shaking to rouse him the second time. A tugging on the wrists told him he was handcuffed, then a cup of cold water was thrown in his face, and it felt good. His tongue licked the liquid off his parched lips. He blinked at the sallow-faced lawman who was dragging him to his feet. Despite his aches and pains he let himself be propelled into the small office adjacent to the cell.

'Sit down,' the lawman told him curtly. 'Before you fall down.'

He sat down on an upright wooden chair facing a solid oak table. The town marshal moved around the table to a well-worn leather armchair that he probably slept in.

'Name?' he enquired.

'Shand . . . Paul Shand,' the young cowboy answered honestly and without guile.

'How much money did you take with you into the card game?' the town marshal asked him.

'Close on a hundred dollars,' Shand told him. 'It was money I'd worked hard for for a long time.'

The lawman stuck a cheroot in his mouth and struck a match.

'Alby said you'd made away with two hundred,' he said. 'But we only found eighty five on you. The lying sonofabitch!'

As he tried to light the cheroot the cowboy noticed his hand shaking. The marshal must have had the same thought, because he reached into a drawer and took out a bottle of bourbon. He took a long, deep draught before replacing the cork reluctantly. Then the street door opened and a huge man came in, ducking his head to avoid hitting it on the woodwork of the frame.

'Is he still breathing?' he asked with a contemptuous glance in Shand's direction. 'I thought you'd killed him last night. You should have left him to me. I could have handled him.'

'He had the drop on you, Mogg, you big ape,' the lawman snapped. 'I just tapped him with my .45. If I hadn't he'd have blown a hole in your guts.'

He smiled thinly at the young prisoner. The

bourbon had steadied his nerves. He was enjoying his moment of power.

'Armed robbery, resisting arrest, threatening the life of a law-officer,' he said. 'Don't sound too good to me, son.'

The young cowboy didn't bother to deny the charges. The room smelt of stale liquor and corruption. Nothing that he said would make any difference. The lawman reached into the drawer again. This time he produced a small tin star and tossed it at the big man.

'Put that on, Mogg,' he said. 'Then get this feller's horse from the stable, and mine too. We're all going riding.'

A small crowd had gathered in the street to watch the cavalcade depart. Two of the card players were there and they couldn't conceal their joy on seeing their enemy manacled and humiliated.

'Run him out of town, Marshal,' one of them yelled. 'Give him something to remember us by.'

'And don't forget the money he owes us,' his companion added optimistically.

They rode directly south towards the border for about eight miles, then the lawman drew rein.

'Help him down, Mogg,' he said. 'This is as far as we go.'

As the big man and the youngster stood facing each other the marshal made a short speech of farewell.

'Since you're a convicted thief,' he said, 'I'm gonna take it that your horse is stolen as well. But I'm gonna let you keep it in return for the eighty-five dollars we found on you. This trail leads to Mexico; they're all horse-thieves down there, so you'll be among friends. Don't ever come back to Twin Springs. Next time I ain't gonna be so generous.'

Still Shand said nothing, but the expression on his face spoke volumes. The big man looked up hopefully at the marshal.

'Okay, Mogg,' the lawman told him. 'But just one.'

The punch landed low down on Shand's ribs and he keeled over, groaning.

'One more, Marshal. Please . . .'

The kick lifted the cowboy a foot in the air and landed him on his back. As he lay there he felt the cuffs being removed from his wrists and then he heard the sound of the horsemen riding off back to town.

TWO

The sun was close to the zenith when Paul Shand caught sight of the rickety signpost that pointed to the south-west. It read simply: TORREVIEJA, and he guessed that somewhere along the route he'd crossed the border into Mexico. Unfortunately, the signpost gave no indication of distance but at least he knew now that he was heading towards a settlement.

Eventually the hilly landscape flattened out into a narrow plain hemmed in by mountain ridges to the east and west. The old church tower that gave Torrevieja its name was visible for miles off and it gave him heart to endure a little longer the numerous aches and pains in his body that were aggravated by the movements of the gelding as it picked up its pace in the hope of finding water in the township.

This Mexican pueblo was twice the size of the town he'd left that morning. There were children playing in the dusty street and old men watched them from the shade while the womenfolk no doubt busied themselves with the household chores indoors. At the entrance to the main street there was a stone well to welcome visitors to the pueblo. One of the youngsters ran over to it before he could dismount and drew up a bucket of cold water for the cowboy and his mount. Shand accepted the gift gratefully; he felt bad that he had nothing to offer the kid in return, but the boy seemed to understand his gesture of apology and flashed a smile that held no regret or malice.

There were at least two cantinas visible already. The nearest of the bars had half a dozen horses tethered outside, and in the interior a piano was being played badly and raucous voices were singing along in English. When the gelding had drunk its fill he led it past the first cantina and on to the second, which was a hundred yards further along the street. It offered a shady spot for the horse and also for himself. When he'd secured the horse to the rail he sat down on the brown earth with his back resting against the woodwork of the saloon. He wasn't feeling so grand, so he closed his eyes and let sleep overcome him, helped by the afternoon heat.

He felt a finger prodding away at his shoulder;

the small lad who'd offered him water was standing over him.

'*Comida*,' the boy said. '*Comida*,' and accompanied the word by making eating gestures with his hands and lips. Shand rubbed his eyes; he wasn't in the mood for games.

'I cain't afford no food,' he told the boy irritably. '*No dinero, comprende*?'

The youngster merely laughed and tugged at his shirt. With a sigh, the cowboy got up and dusted himself down with his Stetson. When he'd finished the Mexican boy tugged his arm and led him through the bead curtain and into the cantina.

A distinguished-looking old gentleman was seated at a table with two other men. They all looked up when Shand came in and nodded their heads to acknowledge his presence. Meanwhile, the plump bartender was placing a bowl of thick broth and several chunks of dark bread on a table in the far corner of the room. He turned and addressed the newcomer in Spanish.

'*Venga, señor. Coma*,' he invited him. '*Lo paga el señor*.'

As he spoke, the young boy pointed a hand in the direction of the elderly gentleman, who was watching them with interest. Paul Shand understood that the meal was for him and that it was paid for.

'I . . . I've no money,' he stammered in English.

The old Mexican gentleman merely smiled at him.

'I do much business with Americans,' he replied in English. 'Some are good to me; they give me help. For that, now I help you, *señor.*'

Shand mumbled a word or two of thanks; he was surprised and embarrassed by this upturn in his fortunes, but he needed no further encouragement to sit down at the table and start eating. It was the first proper meal he'd had in days. The Mexican lad withdrew discreetly and the three Mexicans resumed their conversation and left their guest in peace. Meanwhile, the bartender was drawing him a cold beer to accompany the tasty beef stew he'd been regaled with.

He was still eating when the street outside was filled with the sound of whooping, yelling and the clatter of horses' hoofs. The bartender grinned over at the cowboy and explained:

'Gringos . . . locos!'

Shand realized that what he could hear was the departure of the Americans who'd been drinking in the other cantina. The street children were shouting their goodbyes in Spanish; it was all very good natured. After all the excitement comparative calm returned to the street; then, a few minutes later, the bead curtain was thrust aside and a stranger walked, or rather staggered, into the saloon. He was no older than Paul Shand but his face was lined with experience. He looked what he was – a gunslinger. When he addressed the bartender his voice slurred a little.

'Gimme whiskey,' he snapped. 'A bottle . . . pronto!'

The bartender looked none too pleased to see him. The newcomer's face was scowling and the two Colts hanging low at his hips were a further warning to be careful. He ignored the glass he was offered and took a long swig from the bottle. Then his gaze swept the room contemptuously.

'Know something?' he announced. 'I can outshoot any dam' greaseball in this town.'

He stared provocatively at the three middle-aged Mexicans and they averted their eyes diplomatically. The gunslinger was obviously bent on trouble. Paul Shand glanced across at the bartender, who was looking distinctly uneasy. Fortunately, at least for the moment, the man at the counter seemed content that his challenge had been declined and had turned his attention back to the whiskey.

As he drank a single rider was making his way along the main street towards the cantina. When he reached it, he dismounted and strode purposefully inside. He was a fellow in his mid-thirties but his physique was that of a younger man. When he addressed the gunslinger it was almost with disdain.

'When Parsons noticed you weren't with us, he sent me back for you,' he said. 'If I was you I'd shift my ass now.'

The youngster's face grew even more surly.

'You go tell Parsons to go to hell,' he retorted. 'Tell him I'm quitting. I've quit.'

'Don't be a dam' fool,' the older man said. 'The boys didn't mean no harm. You're new to the gang, that's all. That's why they all kid you.'

'They was pushing me around, Mantle,' the young gunslinger replied. 'And I won't stand for it. Not from Parsons, not from you, not from nobody. They was lucky I didn't kill one of them.'

'Sure, kid,' Mantle agreed. 'Well, I'm gonna wait for you out in the street. If you ain't out in five minutes I'll let Parsons know what you said.'

'Dam' right, Mantle,' the gunslinger said. 'You and him can go to hell together.'

Paul Shand was sorry to see Mantle go. He'd seemed confident of his ability to handle the young drunk. Shand was weary but he couldn't relax while the gunslinger was still there.

The three Mexicans had begun to talk again amongst themselves. They, too, wanted to return to normality. Unfortunately, the youngster at the counter had other ideas.

'You greaseballs better stop talking about me like that,' he warned them suddenly and the three of them froze.

At that point Shand got up from his table, making sure that he made plenty of noise as he did so. Anything to distract the gunslinger's attention from the Mexicans. He could feel his pulse racing, as it always did when he found himself in this sort of situation, but his muscles were loose and supple. He'd learned to use a gun from a tender age; his father had made sure of that. The gunslinger swung round to face him.

'What's wrong?' he asked. 'You a friend of those greaseballs?'

Shand thought of the food and drink he'd just consumed.

'Yeah,' he said. 'I guess I am. You got a friend, too. He's waiting for you outside.'

Under normal circumstances the gunslinger would have wondered about the qualities of anyone willing to face up to him, but by now the whiskey had got the better of him. His usual self-confidence had become rashness; his mind was fuddled yet to him he seemed to be thinking with unusual clarity; his reactions were dulled, yet he felt that he was razor-sharp.

'You'd better sit back down, mister,' he told Shand. 'You just ain't good enough.'

As he spoke his left hand moved towards the bottle on the counter. But it was the other hand Shand was watching. As it dropped on to the handle of the Colt, Shand drew smoothly and blew a hole in the gunslinger's chest from less than fifteen feet.

Nobody in the bar moved or spoke for a few moments, and then the bead curtain moved again and the man called Mantle reappeared in the doorway.

THREE

Paul Shand wasn't going to take any chances, so he kept his .45 in his hand in case Mantle had thoughts of vengeance on his mind. However, the gunslinger seemed calm enough as he turned to the small group of Mexicans and addressed them in halting Spanish. When he'd finished speaking the gentleman who'd treated Shand to his meal replied in English.

'There is no necessity to apologize, *señor*,' he assured the American. 'I have met your Señor Parsons more than once. He is always correct when he visits Torrevieja, and his companions also.' He glanced disapprovingly at the dead man. 'But this man was an exception,' he went on. 'He wished for trouble. It was not the fault of the *señorito*; he defended himself, nothing more.'

Mantle nodded his head and turned back to face Shand, who was slowly replacing his gun in its holster. Behind the counter the bartender gave a relieved smile as he felt the tension drain from the air.

'I cain't leave him here like this,' Mantle told the young cowboy. 'Will you help me carry him out to his horse?'

Shand nodded; Mantle's gaze was without guile, and he was prepared to trust him now.

'Sure,' he agreed. 'I guess I owe you that.'

The corpse was surprisingly light, as if all the blood had flowed out of it. They had no difficulty in raising it on to the horse that was tethered outside the cantina. Mantle secured it with rope and then got on his own bay mare.

'D'you live in this pueblo?' he asked suddenly.

'Nope,' Shand answered. 'I only crossed the border this morning from Twin Springs.'

'Twin Springs . . .' Mantle looked interested. 'What sort of place is it? D'you know it well?'

'Well enough not to go back there,' the cowboy admitted with a rueful smile. 'The marshal there promised to string me up if I ever do.'

Mantle stared at him in astonishment.

'The marshal of Twin Springs was good enough to run a feller like you out of town?' he said. 'That ain't the picture I got of him.'

'It wasn't just the marshal,' Shand replied. 'I made plenty of enemies in a short time.'

The gunslinger laughed, but at the same time

he was observing the young cowboy closely. Shand looked pretty much down on his luck.

'We're camped three miles west of Torrevieja,' Mantle said. 'We'll be there till sun-up tomorrow. We're one man short, thanks to you. If you fancy joining us, you'll be welcome. Think about it.'

'What if your Mr Parsons don't think like you do?'

'He will,' Mantle assured him. 'Parsons don't make many mistakes, but the feller you killed sure was one of them. He ain't gonna be missed or grieved over. By the way, what's your name?'

'Shand.'

The gunslinger reached into his breast-pocket and took out a couple of silver coins.

'Take them,' he told the young cowboy. 'I'd rather you join us because you want to than 'cos you're stony-broke. Remember: you got till sun-up tomorrow to decide . . .'

As it turned out he didn't have to wait that long. The sun was sinking behind the western horizon when Paul Shand rode the chestnut gelding into the encampment Mantle had spoken about. Before he got within a hundred yards of the camp-fire a tall, angular man detached himself from the shadow of a massive boulder and covered him with his rifle.

'Git your hands up, young feller,' he ordered, though he couldn't have been much older than thirty himself. 'Ride on real slow till I tell you to stop.'

Shand did exactly as he was told. He'd asked Mantle no questions about the gang's activities, but he could guess that they were on the wrong side of the law. Men like that lived on their nerves; one false move and he'd end up with lead poisoning.

He was pleased to see the familiar figure of Mantle seated within a couple of yards of the fire. Other men were lying close by on blankets, no doubt sleeping off the effects of the liquor they'd consumed in Torrevieja that afternoon. Next to Mantle sat a grey-bearded feller who looked at least a decade older; he didn't move when Mantle got up to greet the newcomer.

'It's okay, Mitch,' Mantle told the man with the rifle. 'This is the cowpoke Shand I was telling you about. He's the one who gave us all that spade-work.'

Mitch laughed drily; he didn't seem to have minded the extra toil. Shand dismounted and Mantle shook his hand.

'This here's Captain Parsons,' Mantle informed the visitor with a gesture in the direction of the bearded man. 'He's boss around here.'

Parsons responded to the introduction by spitting into the heart of the fire. Still he didn't move.

'I'm pleased to meet you, Captain,' Shand said stiffly. 'Mantle told me about you.'

'Call me Parsons,' the gang-leader told him. 'Mantle was a sergeant in my company and he ain't never forgot it. Anyways, we lost the dam' war so my rank don't mean a thing no more.'

He still sounded sore about it, though the war had ended over twelve years before. Shand was quite happy to change the subject.

'Mantle said you might be needing an extra hand,' he said. 'I guess he told you what happened in the saloon.'

'Yip,' Parsons said. 'He's told me how good you are with a gun, but I still want to know more about you.' His eyes narrowed as he spoke. 'We just buried one maverick; I don't want to take on no more like his kind. In our line of business we gotta be able to trust our pardners, d'you understand?'

'I understand,' the young cowboy assured him. 'I'll tell you anything you want to know. Come to think of it, I ain't got an awful lot to hide.'

As they jawed the three sleeping gunslingers woke up one after the other. They were bleary eyed and parched and Mantle busied himself with keeping them supplied with fresh coffee. None of them was much older than Shand; two of them, Dixon and Hunt, were medium height and stocky and the third, Fenton, was slim and almost as tall as Mitch, the man who'd escorted him into the camp.

Shand's account of his misfortunes in Twin Springs was honest enough to bring a smile to Captain Parsons' lips.

'You really walked into it there,' he chuckled. 'They really saw you coming.'

'You're right,' the cowboy admitted. 'It's the most expensive mistake I ever made.'

Later on, before bedding down for the night, Paul Shand accompanied Mantle down to the arroyo to water the horses.

'You reckon I'm in?' he enquired, since the gang-boss had given him no formal word of acceptance.

'You were in before Parsons even met you,' Mantle replied with a hint of pride in his voice. 'Him and me don't disagree often.' He stared closely into the cowboy's face as he asked; 'How does it feel to rub shoulders with a bunch of outlaws?'

'Yesterday I'd have steered well clear of you,' Shand admitted with a wry smile. 'But why should I respect the law when it's cheated me out of everything I had?'

'You're right,' Mantle agreed. 'Most lawmen ain't no better than we are.'

Shand thought for a moment.

'Tell me,' he said suddenly. 'Why was Parsons so interested in what happened to me in Twin Springs?'

'It ain't *what* happened, it's *where* it happens,' Mantle explained. 'Twin Springs is the next place Parsons is planning to hit.'

FOUR

It was strange finding himself back in Twin Springs just three days after being run out of town. Even the palomino he was riding seemed nervous. The captain had lent it to him, because it was the fastest horse the gang possessed. Mantle reckoned that Parsons was a master of strategy. Well, sweating under his Stetson Paul Shand hoped the outlaw leader had planned it right this time.

His own horse was tied to the rail of the saloon and the others were tethered near the bank they planned to rob that afternoon. None of the gang was visible on the main street. As the palomino ambled slowly along it, Shand hoped he'd have some warning before the gunplay started.

Standing at the window of the adobe jailhouse the giant called Mogg blinked his eyes in disbelief. He waited a moment or two to make sure it wasn't a mirage, then he called out excitedly to the marshal, who was dozing the summer heat away in his leather chair:

'Marshal, it's that sonofabitch Shand, and he's riding a different horse again!'

The lawman jumped to his feet and ran over to the window.

'Well, I'll be a crow's foot!' he exclaimed. 'So he is a horse-thief after all. The varmint sure has some gall.'

When Shand saw the door of the jail swing open he didn't wait around. He spurred the palomino into a gallop and made straight for the hills on the horizon. The chase was on.

Meanwhile, the young outlaw called Dixon was pushing his way through the swing-doors of the saloon. Four old-timers were playing poker at a table near the counter and he made sure to pass close to them as he approached the bartender. Parsons was already at the counter, cradling a glass of beer in his left hand. Dixon didn't even spare him a glance, but did show some interest in the card-game nearby. Sure enough, a minute or so later one of the old-timers stood up and politely invited the youngster to take his place with his back to the bar.

'That's mighty friendly of you, mister,' Dixon thanked him. 'I do enjoy a game, though I guess I ain't much good at it.'

The man opposite introduced himself as Alby and told him:

'You deal, young feller. See if you cain't change my luck.'

Parsons sipped his drink slowly, keeping one eye on the game and the other on the bank, which was visible through the front window. Hand followed hand, with Dixon holding his own and even picking up a few dollars here and there by bluffing. Parsons watched Alby's finger movements every time Dixon picked his cards up. As Shand had predicted the number and position of the old-timer's fingers changed with each deal; they were setting Dixon up.

Suddenly, Dixon reached into his pocket and took out a bundle of bank-notes. He bid ten dollars to start and obviously intended to up the stakes. Parsons saw Alby lay two fingers on the table; Dixon was bluffing again with a mere pair in his hand, and every player at the table knew it. Sure enough, they rose to the bait and the betting was brisk; there was well over a hundred dollars in the pot when Alby finally called the young gunslinger to account.

'I got a flush,' Dixon informed him cheerfully. 'A straight flush.'

The silence was audible as the old-timers digested his statement. The hand he claimed to be holding was unbeatable. Alby was the first to speak.

'Just lay your cards on the table where we can all see them,' he said menacingly. 'We ain't gonna get taken for no ride.'

He stopped speaking as he felt the barrel of a gun pressing against his temple. Nobody had noticed Parsons slide imperceptibly amongst them.

'You wouldn't be calling my friend a cheat, would you?' he asked sternly. 'You must have evil minds to doubt a gentleman's word like that.'

Dixon stood up and drew his Colt to cover the bartender, who was looking quite restless. The man got the message; he stood perfectly still and kept his hands well in sight above the counter.

'You gather all that money up and hand it to my pardner,' Parsons ordered. 'And be glad I ain't going straight to the town marshal and tell him what a wicked old bunch you are.'

Alby did as he was told, but Parsons was more interested in the street outside. Figures were emerging from the doorway of the bank and making for the horses.

'Let's get going,' he told Dixon, then added for the benefit of the rest of them:

'Anyone running out after us gets a bullet in the guts,' he warned as he backed out towards the swing-doors.

This time there was no lawman to hinder his escape. With Dixon keeping an eye on the façade of the saloon, Parsons surveyed the street. The other outlaws had their horses ready for them, but there were a handful of townsfolk out on the street. Parsons fired twice close over their heads to scatter them and the rest of the gang responded with a fusillade designed to discourage people from rushing out of the buildings to see what was going on. It had all been so easy; a few seconds later they were whooping their way out of town and heading for safety.

The town marshal and Mogg were no longer certain who was the hunter and who was the prey. They'd pursued Paul Shand several miles out of town until he'd taken refuge among the crags high above the trail. He obviously knew the terrain quite well since he'd managed to hide the palomino up there with him. Now, from way above their heads he forced his pursuers to take cover as well as he peppered the rocks around them with sporadic rifle shots that never missed by more than an inch or two. Soon the marshal was forced to conclude that the misses were deliberate; for some reason Shand was content to pin them down so that progress upwards was impossible, while at the same time any attempt by them to turn tail and ride off would be fool-hardy.

'Dammit, Mogg,' the lawman snapped irritably.

'This is a fine mess you've gone and landed us in.'

The big man's mouth gaped wide. All he'd done had been to stand at the jailhouse window and report what he'd seen. All the rest had been up to his companion.

'Hold on, Marshal,' he protested feebly. 'I was just following you.'

The lawman wasn't listening; a cloud of dust in the distance back along the trail told him that they'd both been followed. He surmised that some of the townsfolk had formed a posse to help them out. All was not lost.

'Just keep that fool head of yours out of his rifle sight, Mogg,' he said with a grin. 'We'll soon have plenty of men to flush him out into the open.'

But when the riders drew near he was surprised to see that they were all strangers to him. Nevertheless, he called out a warning to them from his hiding-place.

'You'd better take cover, friends,' he yelled out to them. 'We gotta horse-thief cornered up there and he's fighting for his life.'

The men dismounted nonchalantly and their bearded leader ambled over to where the two men were crouched.

'Don't you fret yourselves none about Shand,' Parsons told them. 'He's just a young kid who's playing games with you.'

The town marshal stiffened. Some of the newcomers had drawn their Colts.

'You get rid of your guns before you talk to the captain,' Mantle advised the two townsmen. 'And make it real slow, so there's no risk of an accident.'

Nobody had raised his voice but the atmosphere was menacing. The lawman drew his gun very carefully and let it drop on the brown earth. Mogg was even more cautious; he unbuckled his whole gunbelt and threw it away from him with a flourish. Both men could feel the cold sweat of fear on their bodies.

'You fellers have got Shand all wrong,' Parsons informed them. 'The kid ain't no horse-thief. That's my palomino he's riding. Now would I be fool enough to lend him my own horse if I thought he was a thief?'

He stared at each man in turn and they shook their heads vigorously. He continued speaking in the same, measured tone: 'So when you made Shand pay for that horse a few days ago, he was buying something he already owned by rights. Which means you still owe him the price of a horse, Marshal.'

The lawman lowered his gaze like a scolded child.

'I . . . I guess I was hasty, Captain,' he conceded. 'I ain't got the money with me, but I can get it from my office for you.'

A couple of the outlaws laughed ironically at his words and Parsons beckoned Fenton to step forward.

'Take one of the horses,' he told him. 'We can always use a spare.'

Fenton took hold of the horse nearest to where the town marshal was standing. It was a good-looking filly and it had probably cost him a few months' wages.

'That's one thing settled then,' Parsons commented with satisfaction. 'And cheer up, Marshal; you still got money to buy yourself another horse.'

He turned towards the big man, Mogg. Everyone else seemed to he enjoying the joke at the lawman's expense, so Mogg managed to raise a treacly smile to ingratiate himself with the gang leader. He stopped smiling when he saw that Parsons' eyes had narrowed.

'And you are the feller who gave our pardner a beating,' Parsons said.

Moving smoothly as a snake, Mitch closed on the big man. He'd drawn both his guns and he thrust one of them up under Mogg's chin. The big man was pressed backwards against a rock, and when he stretched out a hand to steady himself Mitch pinned it to the rock with the other six-shooter.

'I'm gonna give you what you never gave Shand,' Parsons told him. 'A choice. Now, where do you want it – in the neck or in the hand?'

From his hiding-place among the boulders Paul Shand heard the shot ring out, followed by the tortured screaming of the stricken towns-man. He peeked down and saw the big man writhing in agony, with blood pouring from his shattered limb. Far from being exultant, Shand felt a sinking feeling in his gut. The sound of laughter rang in his ears. What had he let himself in for?

FIVE

The successful milking of the bank at Twin Springs had left the outlaw gang in good spirits, and they endured the week-long trek westwards without complaining. Whether the sun beat down on them unmercifully or summer storm clouds drenched them to the skin they smiled through it all and recounted anecdotes; the older members recalled their exploits in the Civil War, while the youngsters, not to be outdone, spoke of the escapades in their early teens which had embarked them on their present life of banditry. Only Paul Shand remained quiet and subdued, speaking only when spoken to, and contributing nothing to the general conversation of the gang.

Mantle was more aware than most of the newcomer's low spirits and he waited for the chance to take him to one side and have a long talk with him. That chance came when Parsons ordered Shand to take the first watch one night when they were camped among hills the outlaw leader thought might be the haunt of Apache Indians. Mantle waited until everybody seemed to be asleep, then he rose silently from his blanket and went across to where Shand was standing, some fifty yards from the camp itself.

They stood side by side for a few moments, watching the pattern of stars in the clear firmament overhead. Even then Shand didn't say a word, so the older man decided to take the initiative.

'You've changed, kid,' he remarked. 'You ain't been the same person since we hit Twin Springs. What's wrong? Don't you reckon Parsons played square with you?'

The young cowboy's face was clearly visible in the moonlight. He looked tense and unhappy.

'It ain't nothing like that, Mantle,' he said. 'Parsons gave me what he took from the gamblers who cheated me. I ain't no worse off than when I started, so I got no grumbles on that score.'

'What is it then?' Mantle persisted.

The young cowboy didn't reply; there was no way he'd have known where to begin. But Mantle was determined to make him get it off his chest.

'You didn't like what they did to the big feller, did you?' he said. 'You didn't think it was right.'

'Nope, I guess I didn't,' Shand admitted. 'I seen

bad things before, but nothing like that, not in cold blood.'

'It was revenge,' the older man explained. 'It was to pay Mogg back for what he did to you. When you joined us the captain became responsible for you, just like he was responsible for his unit in the old days.'

'He should have given me the chance to get even with Mogg,' Shand replied. 'He wouldn't have been so brave facing me man to man.'

The experienced gunslinger chuckled at his young friend's naïvety.

'Like in them fool countries where they have duels and things?' he asked incredulously. 'D'you think that's what's gonna happen to us when we get hunted down? D'you think some lawman's gonna hand your gun back to you and tell you to walk ten paces and turn and fire at him? The heck he will; there'll be a lynch-mob waiting to string us up, and the only lucky break we'll get is if the rope breaks our necks when we drop instead of just hanging there for ages choking to death!'

Paul Shand listened to his stark, chilling speech in silence. In the stillness of the night it was almost like a prophecy.

'I'll get over it,' he told his companion quietly.

'Well, you'd better make it fast,' the gunslinger warned him. 'The boys don't like you moping around like this. They'll get to saying you're some sort of jinx, and then they'll start thinking of ways to get rid of you. . . .'

Shand took the warning seriously and from the very next day he became much more sociable, if only on the surface. Then, one day he awoke to find that Parsons and the gunslinger called Mitch were nowhere to be seen. It was the young outlaw Hunt who explained the situation to him as he brewed an early coffee on the camp-fire.

'They've gone on a reconnoitre,' he said. 'That's Parsons' way. He'll hang around a town for a couple of days, just watching and listening. He's on the look-out for any weaknesses before he decides if it's worth the risk of moving in on the place.'

'Why Mitch?' Shand enquired. 'I thought Mantle was closest to him.'

'They're both close to him,' Hunt replied, 'but Mitch is our fastest man on the draw. Mantle's good enough, but Mitch is the sharpest I've seen. Mantle wouldn't live with him; none of us would.'

Dixon raised his head from his blanket; he'd done a long watch and was enjoying a lie-in. He'd been listening to their conversation, as had Mantle and Fenton from a greater distance away. Dixon was eager to make a point.

'Don't write off the feller you're talking to, Hunt,' he said. 'Shand did outdraw Coleman, remember?'

Shand's face flushed as he thought back to the incident in Torrevieja that had launched him on his present course.

'I ain't nothing special,' he said defensively. 'God knows what he'd had to drink that day. He could hardly stand, but still he drew on me.'

Mantle was listening to him approvingly. He liked Shand and felt almost responsible for his well-being since he'd introduced him to the gang. He didn't want any stupid rivalries over reputations growing up between him and the established members of the gang. He ambled over to help himself to some coffee.

'Shand's right,' he agreed. 'He wouldn't have taken Coleman if Coleman had been sober, but at least he had the guts to stand up to a bully. I guess that's all the captain expects of any of us: the guts not to back down.'

The younger gunslingers nodded their heads thoughtfully. Mantle was more experienced than they were, and he'd put things into perspective. Nobody ought to challenge anybody for supremacy; that was the mistake Coleman had made, and he'd paid heavily for it. Fenton came over to join them and make sure he wasn't missing out on the coffee. It was he who had the last word on the subject.

'I never did like Coleman much,' he said, and spat cheerfully into the flames. 'I ain't gonna miss him one goddamn bit.'

*

It took Parsons and Mitch less than two days to complete their reconnaissance mission, then they returned to base, looking well satisfied with themselves. Before giving a report to the whole group Parsons confided his thoughts to his closest partner, Mantle.

'There's a town called Larkwood less than half a day's ride away,' he told him. 'It's in Arizona Territory. It's a sleepy kind of place, but all that's set to change. They've found copper in the hills to the north and the stores and the two saloons in Larkwood are starting to do good business each time the miners get paid. It's a township that's been dead, but it's started to spring to life again. At the moment it's still peaceful and law-abiding. It's a good place to clean out before somebody else gets the same idea.'

'What about the law?' Mantle asked. 'There must be a sheriff or a marshal in a frontier town.'

'They got a town marshal called Powell,' Parsons answered. 'He's been in a few rough places as a deputy – Laramie, Cheyenne, Tucson; but he's long in the tooth now, kinda looking forward to his retirement.'

Mantle was looking very pensive. It sounded a good prospect at the present time. Eventually things would have to change; money invariably led to trouble and the good citizens of Larkwood would have to face up to reality.

'Where are we gonna hit them?' he enquired.

'The bank,' Parsons said. 'It's an old building and they ain't never known trouble in living memory. The owner likes a drink and a game of dice at noon, and the town marshal always joins in. They cain't even see the bank from the saloon they use every day.'

He sounded very relaxed and confident. He'd found out a lot of information in a short time. Mantle wondered if the captain had met some old acquaintance in Larkwood. Parsons had had a chequered career and he often ran into men he'd known in the past, especially former Confederate soldiers.

'When d'you intend to strike?' Mantle asked.

'Soon. The miners hit town last weekend and the business folk must have put plenty of money in the bank by now. The building must be bulging. I'm aiming for speed so that it'll all be over before anyone realizes what's going on.'

'Are we all going in?' Mantle asked. 'Or is somebody gonna stay behind with the loot from Twin Springs?'

'I've thought about that,' Parsons told him. 'I ain't made up my mind yet about that new feller Shand. I don't know how he'll be if things get tough. I don't trust him enough to take him in with us. He can stay behind.'

Mantle stared at the gang boss. He didn't understand his logic.

'If you don't trust him,' he said, 'how come you're gonna let him guard the money we took?'

'I've talked it over with Mitch,' Parsons told him. 'You're gonna stay behind as well, to keep an eye on the kid.'

The three younger outlaws, Dixon, Hunt and Fenton, kept their eyes peeled as they rode into Larkwood with the sun blazing directly overhead. It was a good time for visiting since the street was empty, the residents having chosen to remain indoors to stay cool. Parsons and Mitch had preceded them into the town and were watering their horses at the stream that skirted the perimeter of the buildings.

It was because the main street and the rest of the township roughly followed the curved course of the stream that the bank was not visible from the saloon where the banker regularly met the town marshal and other friends for an amicable game of dice or cards.

The gunslingers dismounted casually some twenty yards from the bank and walked towards its entrance. Despite their apparent nonchalance their pulses were racing as always happened when action loomed. Fenton glanced around and saw Parsons and Mitch leading their horses up a side road in the direction of the bank. The captain nodded his head to indicate that all was well, and Fenton muttered a few words to his companions. The three of them pulled their neckerchiefs up over the lower half of their faces and strode purposefully into the building.

There was one woman customer at the counter and only one cashier on duty. Hunt walked past the customer and poked his Colt into the cashier's chest; there wasn't even a glass screen to contend with.

'Money,' he said. 'Pronto!'

The cashier was not a young man, and all the colour drained from his face. Meanwhile, Dixon had jumped nimbly over the counter. He drew his six-gun and kicked open the door leading to an inner office. A man with a greying handlebar moustache looked up in astonishment from a ledger that lay open on the desk in front of him. Dixon pointed the gun at his head.

'Open the safe and fill this,' he ordered, throwing the man the rolled-up sack he'd brought with him. 'You've got one minute.'

The man fixed him with a stare that was full of distaste, but he rose to his feet and went over to the squat iron safe in the corner of the room. He fiddled with the key and the door swung open. Before he could put his hand inside Dixon struck him a heavy blow on the side of the head and sent him reeling to the floor.

Outside the building the two older gunslingers were managing to look relaxed and natural in case anyone was watching them from one of the windows of the houses opposite. Then, of all things, they heard the sound of horsemen approaching and a troop of blue-uniformed soldiers appeared around the bend in the road. It was the last thing they expected to see, but both outlaws kept their cool.

'Get inside,' Parsons told his companion. 'Keep them in there till they've gone by.'

Of course, he couldn't be sure that they would ride past without stopping, but he trusted to his luck, and it held. The soldiers went by with hardly a glance in his direction and jingled and jogged their way into the distance. He poked his head inside the bank.

'You finished?' he asked and the assembled outlaws nodded their heads, their guns still pointed at the cashier behind the counter. Then the door of the inner office swung open and the injured man appeared, the side of his head seeping blood. He raised the pistol he was carrying and fired it wildly without taking proper aim. The lady customer started screaming hysterically and Parsons returned the fire as his companions hurried past him and out on to the sidewalk. Parsons slammed the door behind him just in time as a slug thudded into its woodwork.

He didn't need to shout any instructions to his men; the troopers had halted in their tracks a couple of hundred yards away. They'd heard the shots or the screams, or both. Some of them had already drawn carbines from their scabbards. The outlaws were all mounted by now and a couple of them, Mitch and maybe Fenton, loosed off a couple of warning shots with their .45s, just to discourage the bluecoats.

The tactics only worked for a few seconds and the cavalrymen soon recovered their discipline and poise. They'd spent weeks hunting Apaches in the wilderness and they weren't going to be scattered by a bunch of bank-robbers.

Parsons heard a yelp close by. Dixon, who'd been holding the money sack, had had his hand shattered by a rifle-shot and the sack had fallen to the ground.

'Forget it,' Parsons shouted at him. 'Let's save our goddamn skins!'

Dixon gritted his teeth and hung on for dear life. At least the gang leader had prepared them for this sort of mishap; in case of trouble they knew they were to rendezvous at a location well away from where they'd left Mantle and Paul Shand. There was no point in leading pursuers towards the cache of stolen dollars.

And then the fleeing outlaws had a stroke of luck. As the leading soldier approached the bank a man stumbled out of the building and staggered across his path. There was no way the trooper could avoid him, though he reined the horse in hard. As the man fell under the hoofs of the charging animal the horse stumbled and fell into the path of other pursuers and in a matter of moments the ground was littered with fallen riders and their hapless steeds.

SIX

Mantle and Paul Shand waited with growing uneasiness for the return of their fellow outlaws from the raid on Larkwood. They had been left in charge of the spare horse and the money taken from the bank at Twin Springs, and they were installed in a rocky recess that overlooked the trail leading directly south from Larkwood to the Mexican frontier.

By sundown Mantle had to admit that something had gone seriously wrong with the raid.

'They oughta be back here by now,' he muttered morosely. 'Surely one of them must have got away.'

'If they are on the run, this is the last place they'll head for,' the younger man pointed out logically. 'They won't want to lead a posse in our direction, not with what we've got with us.'

His comment cheered the gunslinger up a little.

'I guess you're right, Shand,' he conceded. 'As it is, nobody can link us to the rest of the boys. But if the law does question us, how do we explain away all the money we're carrying?'

Shand mulled it over; his companion was so concerned about the fate of his partners, he didn't seem capable of working out a plan of action.

'Let's hide it in the rocks,' he suggested. 'Then, when we do meet up with Parsons again, we can lead him back here to pick it up.'

The idea appealed to the gunslinger and together they concealed the loot deep beneath a large, flat rock to protect the banknotes from the vicissitudes of the weather. When they'd finished they put together a pile of smaller stones visible from the trail which acted as a pointer to where the cache was buried.

They camped the night in the same place in case any of the outlaws made their way back under cover of darkness, but nobody did turn up. The next morning Shand, who'd slept more soundly than Mantle, was the first awake. Barely were his eyes adjusting to the early morning sunlight when he heard one of the horses neigh in alarm.

Shand threw his blanket to one side and leapt to his feet. A young Indian brave was stealthily leading one of the horses away from the camp. Shand reached down for his Colt and shouted a warning before firing it over the head of the retreating brave. In response the Indian lad jumped nimbly on to the horse's back and spurred it on with his bare feet. By this time the cowboy was tired of playing games; he lowered the Colt a fraction and prepared to shoot to kill, but a searing pain ran through his left side, just below the ribs, and doubled him up helplessly.

Behind him Mantle was also on his feet, and wide awake. Some fifty yards away two mounted Indians were watching him. One of them had just fired the arrow that had incapacitated Paul Shand. Mantle didn't intend to be a sitting target. He raised his six-gun and fired a few shots in their direction and then reached down for his rifle.

The Indians got the message and contented themselves with the one horse their daring had gained for them. They sped away, lying flat on their mounts while Mantle stood there and watched them go. There was no point in wasting any more shells on them. He turned back to where Paul Shand was sitting on the ground, his face bathed in sweat and lined with pain.

'Let me see where they got you,' Mantle said and the young cowboy let his arm drop to the floor.

'It's gone straight into the flesh,' Mantle informed him. 'I guess I could cut it out for you, but I cain't be sure it won't turn bad later on.'

Paul Shand said nothing; his head was bowed and he was feeling lousy. But at least the injury to the young cowboy had focused the gunslinger's mind.

'I'm taking you to a doc,' he informed his companion. 'He can work on you while the wound is still fresh.'

Rose Talbot's thoughts were as black as her clothing as she walked slowly back from Larkwood's Boot Hill, flanked on one side by Mr Toomes, her uncle's chief clerk, and on the other by the town's only attorney, Wilson Emery, who also owned its largest saloon. She was strangely troubled by the thought that Uncle Julian had died because he'd stayed on at the bank at the end of the previous morning to complete some ledger work.

Julian Talbot had dispatched Toomes to the Red Stag saloon to apologize for his absence from the daily card game. Normally it was Toomes who remained in charge at the bank during the midday break, but fate had decided things otherwise. It might well have been her uncle walking at her side on this torrid afternoon, and Mr Toomes lying in his coffin six feet under.

Wilson Emery, tall, elegant and still youthful in appearance despite his forty years or so, kept a protective eye on the young girl as they made their way homewards with a retinue of townsfolk following respectfully behind. The preacher had certainly kept them a long time in the church out of respect for the memory of one of Larkwood's most prominent citizens, but the hardest part had been the time spent standing at the grave-side with the Arizona sun beating down on them like a cascade.

As they walked by the Evergreen guesthouse Rose Talbot hesitated and Emery glanced at her solicitously.

'Are you all right, my dear?' he enquired gently. 'You aren't feeling faint, are you?'

There was almost a note of hope in his voice. He'd have loved the chance to slip his arm around her slender waist and feel her leaning on him for support. But Rose Talbot shook her head and tried to smile to show her gratitude, though her dark eyes were still moist with tears.

'I expected Mrs Field to be at the church or the cemetery,' she said. 'She said she'd be there, and she was Uncle Julian's closest friend.'

Mr Toomes coughed respectfully before butting in on their conversation.

'Why don't you call on her, Miss Talbot?' he suggested. 'I'm sure she must have had a good reason for not attending the funeral. Besides, it will do you good to talk to someone like Mrs Field. It will make you feel better.'

The girl turned to the chief clerk and gave him

an even warmer smile than she had the attorney, or at least that was how it seemed to Wilson Emery. He could have given Toomes a good kick when he realized that Rose was detaching herself from the group and starting to cross the road to the guesthouse.

'Don't forget to get in touch with me if you need any help, Rose,' he called after her and she turned her head to answer him.

'Thank you, Mr Emery,' she said. 'I suppose I shall need a lawyer to sort certain things out – things that Mr Toomes can't deal with, I mean.'

'Remember that I am always there for you, my dear,' Emery said, and he shot out his hand and gave her arm a firm squeeze before she could get out of range. 'And don't forget that you can call on me any time at my office or at home.'

He immediately regretted mentioning his home; his wife, Clara, had a sharp tongue and a suspicious mind, especially concerning his lady-friends. However, he could hardly have invited this particular young lady to visit him at the saloon he owned, though he did have a room there kept especially for him to entertain his occasional conquests.

Meanwhile, Rose Talbot had crossed the street and was knocking on the door of the Evergreen guesthouse. She didn't wait for an answer, since the proprietress, Nancy Field, had been almost a

second mother to her over the previous five years.
Rose had moved to Larkwood to live with her
Uncle Julian after both of her parents had
succumbed to a virulent strain of influenza, and
Nancy, who was a close friend of the banker's, had
immediately taken the young teenager under her
wing.

She pushed the door open just as the landlady
was making her way along the downstairs corridor, carrying a jug of cold water in her hands.

'Rose,' Nancy said, 'I was wondering when I'd
get a chance to speak to you. I was on my way to
the church service when the doctor called for me.
There'd been an accident and he needed my help.'

Nancy Field was so good-natured and had
nursed so many friends and relatives in her long
life, that she was always the first person Doc
Gray turned to for assistance.

'A young cowboy was brought in with an arrow
wound,' Nancy continued. 'The doctor wanted me
there when he cut it out, and now we've brought
the young feller here to recuperate. Look, do you
mind taking this water to him?' He's in the back
room. I'm cooking a broth for him and I don't
want it to burn.'

Rose took the jug from her hands. As the chief
clerk had predicted, it was good for her to take
her mind off the funeral for a short while. She
carried the jug along the passageway and into

the sick-room. The curtain had been half-pulled
across to keep the sunlight off the bed, but in the
shade the young man's face struck her as particularly handsome, though it bore a few days' stub-
ble on the chin and the cheeks were drained of
colour because of the ordeal of the surgery.

She went straight to the small table at the side
of the bed and placed the jug next to a glass that
was near empty. There was an upright chair
nearby and she sat down without making a
sound. After a few minutes the cowboy's eyes
flickered open and seemed to fix on her briefly,
but then they closed again with fatigue. Perhaps
she was vulnerable so soon after her bereave-
ment, but whatever the reason she felt a soothing
sense of calm as she contemplated the rise and
fall of the young stranger's chest beneath the
blanket.

She gave a sudden start as the shifting of a
chair told her she wasn't alone in the room. She
turned her head sharply and saw an older man
sitting quietly in one of the darker corners.

'I'm sorry, ma'am,' he apologized. 'I didn't mean
to frighten you. I'm the feller who brought him
in.'

'Oh . . .' Her reverie was broken, but at least
now she might be able to ascertain the identity of
the patient. 'Are you a friend of his?'

'Kind of, ma'am,' Mantle replied cautiously. 'We

was both prospecting in the hills when we met up. That was just over a week ago.'

'And your name is. . . ?'

'Mantle, Brad Mantle, and my pardner's name is Paul Shand. Least, that's what he told me.' He shifted uncomfortably in his chair. 'Mrs Field told me to sit here with him,' Mantle went on, 'though I don't see that I'm doing much good, seeing as how he's asleep most of the time.'

'Why don't you take a break?' the young girl suggested. 'Let me sit with him for a while.'

Mantle wasn't the kind of man who enjoyed sitting around for hours, so he didn't take much coaxing.

'If you're sure you don't mind, ma'am,' he said gratefully.

'I don't mind, Mr Mantle,' she assured him, and she looked as if she meant it.

Paul Shand knew that he'd been pretty poorly. He'd been having recurring dreams about a beautiful young girl who seemed to be caring for him, but when he finally pulled out of the fever it was the gunslinger Mantle who was on watch at his bedside.

'D'you want water?' Mantle enquired and the cowboy nodded his head weakly.

'How long have I been like this?' Shand asked when he'd wetted his throat.

'Two days. How d'you feel now?'

The young cowboy didn't answer the question; there was something else on his mind.

'What about the others?' he asked. 'What happened to them.'

Mantle leaned forward to speak. Although Mrs Field had gone out to the stores, he still didn't want to raise his voice.

'They ran into the US Cavalry,' he said. 'They got away but the soldiers chased after them. Two bluecoats came back this morning with Hunt's horse. Hunt's dead, but there's no news of the others. I guess the soldiers are still on their trail.'

'What are you going to do, Brad?'

'I'll stick around till they come back,' Mantle told him. 'But not here in Larkwood. There's a feller in town I know from somewhere, but I cain't remember where. I don't want him to link me with Parsons.'

Paul Shand's eyes were dull; the fever had drained him.

'I'm quitting, Brad,' he said suddenly. 'Tell Parsons I don't want no part of the money. I'm out . . . finished.'

He didn't know how Mantle was going to take the news. As it was, the gunslinger didn't bat an eyelid.

'Okay, Paul,' he said. 'If I do meet Parsons again I'll square it with him. He won't lose any sleep over it. He never could make up his mind about you.'

Mantle heard the front door open and he rose to his feet.

'I'll be seeing you, Paul,' he said. 'Good luck.'

Out in the corridor he bumped into Nancy Field, who had her hands full with the provisions.

'I cain't hang around town any longer,' he informed her. 'I'll leave you some money, in case my pardner is here for a while.'

'Don't worry on that score, Mr Mantle,' she smiled. 'That side of it has been taken care of; the doctor's bill, too.'

The gunslinger thought immediately of the well-dressed young lady who'd been spending time at Paul Shand's bedside during his illness. If that was the way things were, maybe Shand was quitting the gang at just the right moment. . . .

Brad Mantle had left his horse outside the Frontiersman saloon. From the window of the jailhouse some sixty yards down the road Town Marshal Powell watched his progress with only passing interest. The lawman had heard the story of the two strangers from Doc Gray and there seemed nothing sinister behind their presence in town.

Also watching, from the interior of the Frontiersman saloon, was Con Meadows who did any sort of dirty work that Wilson Emery, lawyer and saloon owner, demanded of him. Meadows remembered Mantle vaguely from his army days. Earlier in the week, when Captain Parsons had paid him for information about the bank, Mantle's name had not been mentioned, but here Mantle was and Meadows thought it one heck of a coincidence that the captain and his former sergeant should be in the same part of Arizona Territory at the same time. However, that wasn't Meadows' problem; after the débâcle of the bank raid, the less he had to do with his old army colleagues, the better.

A buckboard was standing outside the general store right next to Wilson Emery's saloon. As Brad Mantle reached his horse, an attractive, dark-haired woman in her late twenties emerged from the store accompanied by a boy and a girl who couldn't be much older than eight or nine years old. The children clambered up on to the wide bench behind the sturdy pair of horses, but the woman waited for the storekeeper to load the wagon with provisions before she, too, climbed aboard alongside the children.

She was just about to stir the horses into life when a heavily built man came stumbling out of the swing-doors of the Frontiersman saloon, made his way unsteadily around the front of the horses and finally grabbed hold of one of the reins.

'Jack,' the woman protested. 'Let go. I've got to get back to the ranch.'

'And I gotta have money,' he replied, slurring his words as he spoke. 'I need money to get out of this goddamn place and set up someplace else.'

'You've had your money,' the woman told him. 'I even paid you an extra two weeks' wages. You left of your own accord, remember? You left us in the lurch. If you've drunk the money, so be it. I've no more to give you.'

The man pulled savagely on the rein and the horse's head spun round. The animal was starting to get agitated, but the man called Jack just let fly a stream of abuse and invective at the young woman which soon had the little girl by her side weeping with fright.

Mantle didn't really want to get involved, but the child's sobbing made his mind up for him. He walked towards the drunk, whose face was twisted with anger.

'Jack,' he said. 'Why don't you be reasonable and let them go on their way? You ain't doing yourself no good this way.'

The man's eyes narrowed into slits, but he did let go of the rein as Mantle had suggested. Unfortunately, his next move was to drop his hand on to the butt of his .45.

By this time there were several spectators on the sidewalk watching the argument, but nobody saw the short punch Mantle threw, and that included Jack himself, whose jaw took the full impact. The next moment the malcontent was stretched out in the dust and only the occasional groan indicated that he was still alive.

Mantle turned to the young woman on the buckboard.

'You're okay now, ma'am,' he told her reassuringly. 'I'll see to him. If he's got any sense he won't bother you no more.'

The little girl had stopped crying and the boy was staring in fascination at the felled cowboy on the ground. But the woman herself had been shaken up by the incident, more for the children than for herself. She tried to pull on the reins, but her hands were trembling badly and her arms were weak. Then, the door of the jail-house opened further along the street and the town marshal walked out into the sunlight.

Brad Mantle had no desire to talk to him or any lawman.

'If you'll let me tie my horse to the buckboard, ma'am,' he said, 'I'll take over the reins for a while, just until you start feeling yourself again.'

SEVEN

When she'd recovered from her fright the young woman was quite happy to explain to Mantle what lay behind the unpleasant encounter in town.

'Jack Hobbs was foreman at our ranch until he walked out on us just over a week ago,' she said.

'Which ranch is that?' Mantle asked.

'The *Tres Encinas*,' the woman replied. 'That's Spanish for three oaks. My ancestors came to these parts with the very early Spanish settlers. Most people on the ranch and in town call me Sue, but that's short for Susanna – Susanna Johns.'

'Johns doesn't sound very Spanish,' Mantle remarked.

'When my father died, I married the man who was his top hand,' Sue explained. 'I had no brothers, only sisters – and they'd all married and moved on.'

'Your husband shouldn't let you and the kids ride into town alone,' Mantle said. 'Not while that Hobbs feller is nursing a grudge.'

She turned to face him and he was struck by the sad beauty of her eyes.

'My husband was gunned down on the range four years ago,' she said. 'Jack thought he could take his place – in every respect. When he found that he couldn't he took to drink. Eventually he lost the respect of the cowhands. We get some trouble from our neighbouring ranch, Jeff Dickens's spread. It all became too much for Jack to handle, so he quit. You know the rest.'

'Who killed your husband?'

'Marshal Powell looked into it,' Sue replied, 'but he never came up with an answer. Luckily, the children were too young to understand; their father's just a faint memory to them now.'

Mantle smiled at the two kids, who were travelling in silence, listening to every word.

'Is yours a big spread?' he enquired.

'It doesn't need to be. We have some natural springs in the hills, so we're never out of water. Jeff Dickens is an ambitious man; he keeps more stock than his land can feed. That's why he lets them stray on to our pastures.'

They arrived at the ranch house after a two hour drive. It was a nice-looking place set in a grassy valley; the buildings were quite well kept, so obviously some of the cowhands were willing to take orders. They were greeted at the door by a dark-skinned lady whose ample figure was clothed in black. The children came to life when they saw her and they ran with cries of joy into her embrace.

The woman, however, had other things on her mind. She was staring quizzically at the newcomer as if she was trying to assess his qualities.

'Have you found a new foreman, Susanna?' she asked, and the younger woman blushed in confusion.

'No, *Mamá*,' she replied. 'This is Mr . . .' Her voice trailed off, and the gunslinger had to come to her aid.

'My name's Brad Mantle, *señora*,' he said in a formal tone. 'I only just met Sue in Larkwood. She was feeling a little unwell, so I offered to drive her and the children home.'

He felt rather awkward as the lady's head tilted to one side thoughtfully. The two women then exchanged a few words in Spanish. When *Mamá* was satisfied that Susanna was feeling well again, she smiled warmly in Mantle's direction.

'I am grateful to you, Señor Mantle,' she said. 'You must stay and have coffee and something to eat.'

The room he was ushered into was tastefully, if

not expensively furnished. He was left alone for a short time while the women and the children chatted in another room which he assumed was the kitchen. The boy and girl were animated now, and Mantle knew enough Spanish to realize that they were extolling his virtues and telling their grandmother how he'd rescued them from the unwelcome attention of their former ranch foreman. When they all reappeared Susanna was carrying a jug of coffee, the kids had mugs in each hand and the *señora* was holding a large tray of cookies.

As they drank the coffee it was Susanna's mother who did most of the talking. She told him about the five cowhands who worked the spread: Miles who was a friendly soul, but overweight and lazy; he'd got away with murder under Jack Hobbs's stewardship. Then there were the brothers, Max and Pete Thompson, who'd always been cheerful youngsters until they'd fallen for the same girl at the spring barn-dance. Neither of them had won her favour but since then they hadn't spoken to one another and they'd become short-tempered and difficult to handle. The remaining two men, Stewart and Jones, were veteran cowpunchers who, according to the old lady, were no trouble to anyone.

'But tell us about yourself, Señor Mantle,' she urged him. 'Have you done ranch work?'

'I was brought up on a ranch, *señora*,' he

informed her, 'but I only had the chance to do a couple of cattle-drives before the war broke out, and my whole life changed.'

'Are you still a soldier?' the young boy blurted out. 'Do you have a uniform?'

'Nope, I left soldiering when the war was lost,' Mantle said. 'Only I never did go back to ranching, or even think about it.'

'But what about now?' the *señora* asked. 'Do . . .'

'*Mamá*,' Sue Johns said suddenly. 'Do you think Mr Mantle doesn't know where you're leading to?' She raised the jug and refilled the visitor's mug. 'I'm sorry, Mr Mantle,' she apologized. '*Mamá* is going to put you on the spot if you're not careful. It's no secret that we need a ranch foreman, but I'm sure that you've seen and heard too much today even to consider the proposition.'

Brad Mantle looked up at her. She was a very beautiful woman and very vulnerable in her present situation.

'What proposition is that?' he enquired, and as their eyes met she blushed slightly.

To save her further embarrassment he turned away and addressed the older woman.

'I'll accept your offer, *señora*,' he told her. 'But you'll still have to look for someone to do the job long-term. I got commitments, too, and there's no telling when I'll have to quit the ranch for good. . . .'

*

Mantle could hear the sound of hammering coming from the interior of the barn. He crossed the open yard in front of the corral and approached the open doorway. A young cowboy was standing next to a cart, holding a couple of planks in his hands. The man with the hammer kneeling by the side of the cart was an older man, by twenty years maybe. After a few moments both ranch hands became aware of his presence and the hammering stopped.

'Howdee,' Mantle said. 'My name's Mantle. Looks like I'm foreman round here from now on.'

The older cowboy let the hammer fall to the ground; then he rose stiffly to his feet and held out his hand. The man's eyes were sharp and intelligent. He was studying the stranger's hands; they hadn't done any ranch work for years, he could see, but he doubted if they'd been idle either. Mantle's stance was relaxed and confident; whatever his profession he didn't look the kind of man it would be wise to cross.

'I'm Stewart,' the cowpoke said. 'The youngster here is Max Thompson.'

Thompson didn't offer his hand. He was wearing a gun and his look was challenging. Mantle had no reason to push the matter, at least not for the moment.

'I'm told two of the boys are out on the range,' he told the veteran cowpoke.

'That's right,' Stewart replied. 'Jones and Pete Thompson are camped out at one of the watering holes. Pete is Max here's twin brother.'

The younger cowboy's expression grew even more sullen when he heard his brother's name mentioned, but Mantle's mind was on other things.

'That leaves Miles,' he remarked. 'Where's he?'

'Oh, Miles,' Stewart chuckled. 'You could try the bunkhouse, I guess. Miles don't like to venture far when the sun's high.'

'I'll go see if I can rouse him,' the new foreman said mildly. 'I'm sure I can find him something to do around the ranch.'

Expecting to witness some fun, Stewart and Thompson moved to the doorway and watched Mantle cross the yard to the bunkhouse. As he drew near he could faintly hear someone snoring inside. Mantle spotted a large barrel of water standing near the door and he smiled to himself.

The interior of the bunkhouse was dark, cool and spacious. There were five or six two-tiered bunks and Mantle could make out the bulky outline of the missing cowpuncher on the top bunk nearest the door.

'Wakey, wakey, Miles,' he said loudly. 'Time to get up.'

The snoring stopped and the boards creaked as the cowpoke stirred in his bunk.

'Who the hell are you, mister?' he demanded in a thick voice.

'The ranch foreman,' Mantle informed him. 'Now up you get.'

Miles muttered something that sounded very much like: 'Go to hell', and turned over in his bed. Without saying a word, Mantle reached for the Stetson that was hanging on the side of the bunk, took it outside and filled it to the brim with fresh water. A moment or two later the recumbent cowboy was choking and spluttering as the contents of the Stetson hit him full in the face. As he struggled to get up, strong hands dragged him over the side of the bunk and he landed heavily on the earthen floor below.

'You sonofabitch,' he screamed. 'I'll kill you for this!'

Meanwhile, Mantle had retreated out into the yard. The lumbering cowpoke followed him, and blinked in the strong sunlight. His tormentor was right in front of him, grinning like a monkey. Miles threw a haymaker of a right hand, but Mantle was no longer within range. The big cowboy was swung off balance by the force of his own punch and found himself once more on his backside in the dust.

Miles could hear the laughter of the other two

ranch hands as they witnessed his discomfiture. He couldn't contain his anger.

'If I had a gun, I'd kill you right now,' he said through gritted teeth.

Mantle turned to the two spectators by the barn door.

'Get him a gun,' he said calmly, 'if that's what he wants.'

The laughter stopped. The situation had grown serious all of a sudden. Thompson looked questioningly at the older cowpoke. After a moment's hesitation Stewart nodded his head gravely.

By this time Miles had risen to a kneeling position. Max Thompson walked across the yard and tossed his Colt on to the ground within an inch or two of the cowpuncher's right hand.

'Pick it up,' Mantle said, his face quite expressionless.

Miles didn't dare move for fear that the stranger would gun him down.

'I said pick it up, goddamn you,' Mantle repeated. 'That's an order.'

The cowpoke's face was twisted with fear now as he reached tentatively for the weapon. Mantle still hadn't drawn his own gun, or moved his hand anywhere near it.

'You got a gun, Miles,' he said. 'Use it if you want.'

The big man stared into his eyes for a moment

and then he let the gun fall to the floor again. Mantle turned his back on him and walked back towards the other two ranch hands.

'Find him some work to do, Stewart,' he told the older man. 'I'm gonna get acquainted with the layout of the place.'

From her vantage point in the ranch house, Sue Johns had witnessed the whole confrontation. Now she stood at the window and wondered just what kind of demon she'd let out of the gunny-sack.

EIGHT

Wilson Emery was pleased to see that so many of the local businessmen had turned out for the meeting he'd called in Larkwood's courtroom. He considered it natural and right that he should chair the proceedings since he was the township's wealthiest resident. On either side of him at the top table sat Town Marshal Powell and Pritchard, the elderly hardware merchant.

Most pleasing of all was the fact that the lovely Rose Talbot had decided to attend, though she still wore mourning for her Uncle Julian, who'd lost his life trying to foil the bank-raid. Still pale from her ordeal, the young girl looked vulnerable and desirable to the lascivious attorney and saloon-owner. He smiled at her as she passed by, but her eyes were searching for the chief clerk of the bank, Mr Toomes, and she didn't even notice that Emery was watching her. He decided to

show his authority and call the meeting to order;
then Rose Talbot would have to notice him.

He tapped the table sharply with the gavel
that was kept for the use of the county judge who
visited Larkwood occasionally to settle disputes
and dispense justice in cases that lay outside the
town marshal's jurisdiction.

'Friends,' he said condescendingly, 'I've called
this gathering because I know that many of you
are concerned with safety and security in
Larkwood now that it is on the threshold of
unimaginable expansion and prosperity.'

Immediately, a section of the audience began to
shout out suggestions without waiting to be
asked. Wilson Emery was firm with them. Before
they spoke out they should listen to the opinions
of the man in the firing line, Marshal Powell.

The marshal was a lean man in his mid-
forties. He'd been a lawman for most of his working life, and when he addressed the meeting his
tone was measured and sensible. He pointed out
that greater prosperity would mean a greater
temptation for wrongdoers to flood into the
township. Sooner or later the townsfolk would
have to lay out extra money to strengthen its
lawforce, and by that he meant wages for deputy
marshals.

'Get recruiting, then,' one of the storekeepers
yelled out from the back of the hall. 'We'll raise

the money somehow.'

Powell fixed the man with a steady gaze.

'I could go out in the street and pick up three men or more right now,' he said, 'but they would-n't make a lawman between them. A bad deputy is worse than no deputy at all. I've been in towns where the sheriff and his cronies were the citizens' worst enemies.'

Some of the older men present nodded their heads in agreement. You just couldn't rush into something like that. Pin a star on a feller's chest and you could be creating a hero – or a monster.

'I think the obvious cause for concern is the bank,' Wilson Emery said. 'It was only by an incredible stroke of luck that those cavalrymen happened by just when the bank-raid was taking place. Otherwise, the town's investors could all be facing ruin right now.'

His statement really got the hall buzzing and Emery had to resort to the gavel again to establish order.

'I've come up with an idea,' he announced and the audience waited expectantly. 'What we need is a small committee of townsfolk to supervise security at the bank now that Julian is dead. I'd be happy to form such a committee under my own chairmanship.'

All eyes turned to where Rose Talbot and her chief clerk were sitting. The two of them exchanged glances and the clerk shook his head almost imperceptibly. Wilson Emery, sharp-eyed, spotted the movement. He wondered what objection the ornery old fool was going to make to his proposition. In the event it was Rose Talbot who spoke, falteringly at first, but soon gaining in confidence.

'I've discussed the situation with Mr Toomes,' she announced. 'As you probably know by now, I became the new owner of the bank after my Uncle Julian's tragic death.' She stopped to clear her throat. 'I assure you all that I am aware of the dangers Mr Emery has spoken about and the bank is already taking the appropriate measures; Mr Toomes's son, Floyd, is being trained to join the staff. Marshal Powell has also promised to make regular patrols in the vicinity of the bank.'

Her statement gave rise to a heated debate. Some of those present described the measures as feeble and inadequate. Rose Talbot held her ground, and was gratified to find herself supported by old Pritchard, the hardware merchant. But then, Pritchard and Toomes had been friends for years and Pritchard's grandson Jamie and Toomes's boy Floyd were the same age and boon companions. Besides, Pritchard didn't much like Emery, who was a comparative newcomer to Larkwood. Pritchard had built up his business the hard way, whereas it was rumoured that Emery had married his wife Clara for money, not love.

The lawyer found himself outvoted two to one on the top table, since Powell also threw his weight on the side of the bank's new owner, but at least Emery could be satisfied that he'd spread the first seeds of discontent among the town's citizenry. When he called a halt to proceedings he warned that he would be summoning future meetings to give everybody a chance to discuss the changes that were bound to take place in the next few months, or even weeks.

Outside in the street Emery managed to intercept Rose Talbot before the young girl disappeared. Mr Toomes discreetly held back and allowed them to talk. After her performance in the courtroom the chief clerk had no fear that his employer was going to give ground now.

'Those things that I felt obliged to say just now,' Wilson Emery said, laying a protective hand on the girl's shoulder, 'I hope you're not going to take any of them personally, Rose. Your Uncle Julian's death was a terrible loss to the community. God forbid that anything like that should ever happen again. I just urge you to reflect on the feelings of the townsfolk. The security of the bank concerns us all, as citizens of Larkwood.'

Rose Talbot turned and smiled at him, and he

wondered if she had any idea how much her beauty tortured him.

'I'm grateful for your concern, Mr Emery,' she replied. 'But I can't escape my responsibilities, either. That's why I'm listening to the advice given me by my chief clerk and the town marshal. Now, if you'll excuse me, I need to speak to Mr Pritchard about a matter unconnected with the bank.'

'Could it be something that I could assist with?' the lawyer enquired eagerly. It wasn't often that he could get this close to the object of his desires and he wanted to savour the moment a little longer.

Despite her underlying sadness, the girl's eyes sparkled almost playfully.

'Well, if Mr Pritchard can't help me,' she said, 'I promise you'll be the first person I turn to, Mr Emery.'

After a brief word with Mr Toomes, Rose Talbot took her leave of both of them and headed off in the direction of the hardware store that Pritchard ran with the help of his grandson, Jamie. Toomes walked off towards the bank, where he had work to catch up on. Wilson Emery stayed where he was and watched the young girl's graceful movements until she disappeared inside the hardware store. Only then did he turn away and head, not for his office, but the

Frontiersman saloon, which was another of his properties.

The saloon was almost empty at this hour of the day. The bartender and Con Meadows, Emery's right-hand man, were exchanging pleasantries at the counter and Jack Hobbs, formerly the leading hand at the Tres Encinas ranch, was sat in the middle of the room, staring moodily at his empty glass. The bartender broke off his conversation with Con Meadows and moved smoothly along the counter to have a quiet word with the boss.

'Mrs Emery's upstairs waiting for you,' he said. 'She's been there almost an hour.'

The lawyer couldn't suppress a sigh. To be with Rose Talbot one minute and his wife Clara the next was like descending from the sublime to the ridiculous.

'Give me a bottle of rye,' he told the barman.

'There's one up there already,' the man replied, his face expressionless. 'Mrs Emery took it up with her.'

Wilson Emery turned quickly, just in time to catch the gunslinger Meadows with a smirk still on his lips. The lawyer stared at him challengingly but Meadows kept his composure; he knew how heavily the lawyer depended on him to do his dirty work. Emery wasn't going to sack him for mocking his wife, Clara. Emery's gaze swept past him to where Jack Hobbs sat slumped in his chair.

'Is he still here?' he asked irritably. 'Hasn't he run out of money yet?'

'He ran out of money days ago,' the bartender reminded him gently. 'You told me to give him credit, remember?'

Emery had forgotten all about the cowpuncher, what with everything else he had on his mind. He'd told Meadows to look after Hobbs, so he could hardly call the gunslinger out now. The lawyer had thought that maybe the disgruntled ranch foreman could be useful to him some way, but no ideas had developed in his mind. Right now the drunk's presence grated on him.

'Get rid of him,' he snapped. 'Get him off my back. Find him a job – away from here.'

Con Meadows pulled a tobacco pouch from his shirt pocket and started to roll a smoke.

'OK, Mr Emery,' he said amiably. 'I'll find him something useful to do.'

Upstairs in his private quarters Emery found his wife Clara reclining on the velvet-covered *chaise-longue* he'd installed there for his female visitors. The bottle of rye was standing on the dressing-table within arm's reach; it was about half full.

'Disappointed, darling?' she asked as he closed

the door behind him. 'Were you expecting some-one else?'

He could tell the kind of mood she was in and it spelt trouble if he didn't handle her right. Their house was on the periphery of the town and her scenes didn't matter so much there. Here in the saloon they were in the centre of Larkwood and he couldn't afford any scandal.

'The bartender told me you were here, Clara,' he replied with a forced smile, 'drinking. . . .'

She pointed an elegantly varnished fingernail at the rye bottle on the dressing-table.

'I've hardly started, Wilson,' she said. 'Why don't you join me, or are you expecting another visitor?'

He went over to the bottle and poured himself a stiff drink.

'No, nobody,' he told her. 'I came here to work.'

'Not even little Miss Talbot?' she enquired sarcastically. 'Or do you call her Rosie?'

He pushed her legs unceremoniously on to the floor and sat down beside her.

'Don't even mention her name,' he said. 'D'you know what happened just now in that meeting I called about security at the bank? Well, she virtu-ally told me to go to hell.'

'Tut, tut,' Clara said in mock reproach. 'That's not how it looked when you came out of the meeting with her. I happened to be looking out of the window and I saw her turn those big, blue eyes on you, and you just melted on the spot. I almost feel sorry for you at times, Wilson. You're always hankering after something you can't get. And believe me, you'll never have Rose Talbot. You're old and you're slimy and she can read you like a book, which is more than I could do when I was her age, worst luck.'

He didn't want to argue with her, so he did the only thing he knew might work. He laid his hand on her ankle and slowly worked it up the length of the calf and on to the thigh. As he did so, the tension drained from her body and her head fell back on the velvet cushion. Despite everything, he knew the crazy bitch was still in love with him.

'I'll only be a substitute,' she teased him. 'I won't be the real thing.' Then his other hand strayed on to her breast and she began to quiver. . . .

An hour later he went down to the bar to get another bottle of liquor. Now the bartender was the only person in sight.

'Where's Meadows?' Emery enquired.

'He's taken Hobbs over to the Dickens ranch,' the barman told him. 'He said he was going to settle things for you.'

The lawyer nodded his head thoughtfully. That

was one problem solved; but what about the bigger problem reclining on the *chaise-longue* upstairs, drinking rye whiskey as she awaited his return?

NINE

It took Paul Shand almost a week to recover from his fever and feel strong enough to take short strolls along the banks of the stream that had been brought back to life by the seasonal showers. Concerned about his financial obligations he asked the landlady what debts he'd run up during his illness. Nancy Field reassured him straight away, saying that she'd been given money to cover the cost of his board and lodging and also the doctor's fees.

'That sonofagun Mantle,' Shand commented with a shy smile. 'He never told me a thing.'

Mantle had in fact offered to pay for the young cowboy's keep, but as it happened Rose Talbot had got her bid in first. However, Rose had sworn the landlady to secrecy in the matter, so Mrs Field merely smiled back at him.

'You can start paying when you're fit enough to

find work,' she told him, and her statement took him aback. He had no intention of hanging around in Larkwood.

'Work,' he said. 'What work is a cowpoke gonna find in these parts?'

She picked up a feather duster and got to work on the window ledge. Once again Rose Talbot had left it to her to do the explaining.

'Mr Pritchard called here this morning while you were out,' she said. 'He runs the hardware shop in the centre of town. He's looking for someone to help out. There's only him and his grandson Jamie working there, and things have been getting busy since the mines opened up in the hills. If they can't cope, he's afraid someone else may open up another store.'

'But why me?' Shand persisted. 'He doesn't even know me.'

That was the question the landlady had been dreading. She hated telling lies, even when it was for a good cause. She knew Rose Talbot had been working behind the scenes, but once again she'd been forbidden to mention the girl's name. Fortunately, she'd prepared an answer.

'The whole town's heard about you,' she said. 'You were almost killed by the Apaches; that makes you a kind of hero in these parts.'

It was true that children came up to him in the street to ask him to recount his brush with the redskins, but he hardly thought that his wound would stir up much interest among the adult population of Larkwood. Still, a store job did sound lighter work than anything he was likely to be offered on a ranch. It would at least tide him over until he felt strong enough to go back on the trail.

'When do you think I should go and see him?' he asked.

'As soon as possible,' Nancy Field advised him. 'If you commit yourself to working for him he'll give you some more time to get your strength back.'

Pritchard turned out to be a man in his sixties, rather stern in appearance and blunt in his speech. Hopefully, his bark would turn out to be worse than his bite. There was no discussion of terms; he told Shand what he could expect to earn and that was that. The young cowboy accepted at once. The wage was enough to pay for his keep at the boarding-house and also have a few dollars left for himself. Pritchard was very specific on one aspect of the work.

'My grandson Jamie is a good lad,' he said. 'He's strong and he'll do any heavy lifting needed till your wounds heal. I'm employing you because I don't like him handling guns any more than he needs to. Any customer who comes in for a firearm, you or me serve him, understand?'

Shand nodded his head and glanced across at the good-looking teenager who was stacking boxes in the corner of the store. Jamie must have heard his grandfather's words but he showed no reaction at all. In fact, during the whole conversation between Pritchard and the cowpoke he'd only said one word and that was 'howdee' when he was introduced to Paul Shand. But Shand noticed that the youngster's handshake was firm and his gaze deep and steady. He looked a good friend to have, but he wasn't sure what he'd be like as an enemy.

Mr Pritchard asked if Shand could come in to help out the following Saturday if he felt strong enough and the young cowboy nodded his head.

'The miners come in to stock up in the morning before moving on to the saloons,' the storekeeper explained. 'The way them boys drink, it just wouldn't work the other way round. . . .'

Paul Shand's first few hours in the store were just as hectic as they'd promised to be. Old man Pritchard and grandson Jamie had their hands full dealing with the droves of miners who came in demanding shovels, pick-handles and oil-lamps to replace those they'd broken or lost during the previous week.

The young cowboy coped as well as he could, but he did come into his own whenever a customer needed guidance about the suitability of this or that firearm for his own particular needs. Guns were a subject that every cattle drover just had to be familiar with.

By midday the worst of the rush was over; henceforth it would be the turn of the saloon-keepers to reap a harvest out of the visitors. Mr Pritchard was well satisfied with the way the morning had gone.

'You did well, Paul,' he complimented the new employee. 'You didn't let them get to you, however impatient they were. It gets easier as you go along,' he added. 'As I recall, the first ten years were the worst.'

Shand smiled but said nothing. He couldn't imagine himself lasting ten weeks in this kind of work, let alone ten years.

Next it was the turn of the womenfolk of the township and the surrounding area to visit the store in search of pots and pans, brushes and brooms. Some came in alone, some in small groups and some were even accompanied by their reluctant husbands. Shand was in the process of removing some items that had fallen behind the counter when he he heard a girl's voice address-ing him. When he straightened up to see who it was, his face betrayed the shock he felt. The lovely vision he'd seen during his fever was not an illusion but real! For a few moments the words she was uttering didn't register in his brain; she seemed to be asking him about a kettle, but all he could do was stare at her.

'Are you feeling all right?' she enquired anxiously. 'Are you strong enough yet to be working?'

The question brought him back to earth. He was pale and he was feeling tired but he didn't want his employer to think that he wasn't up to the job.

'No, no,' he assured her. 'I'm fine; it's just that I thought that I knew you from somewhere.'

She smiled at him and all his tiredness evaporated.

'I sat with you sometimes when you were ill,' she told him. 'Nancy Field is like a mother to me. She didn't want you to be left alone when you were feverish, but naturally she couldn't be there all the time. Occasionally I'd take over from her. You were so ill, I didn't think you'd remember me.'

Remember her . . . The memory of that face had haunted him ever since. Now he just stood there, unable to think of anything to say. As they stared at one another, Jamie Pritchard brought a couple of copper kettles over and placed them on the counter between them.

'Here you are, Paul,' he said with a mischievous grin. 'This is what Rose came in for.'

His intervention broke the spell and soon the

young lady was on her way, carrying the utensil she'd purchased, but somehow the grin on Jamie's face seemed to last almost until his grandfather closed the shop towards dusk.

'When Paul Shand got back to the boarding-house there was no meal waiting for him as he'd expected. The other lodgers had already eaten and were out on the town. It was Saturday night and Larkwood's main street was full of bustle and life.

'You go and get washed and shaved,' Nancy Field told him. 'I've been invited to eat at a friend's place this evening. When I told her I'd have to cook for you, she said to bring you along as well.'

He shook his head; he'd had a busy day and he didn't feel like going out.

'I'll stay put,' he informed the landlady. 'I won't starve if there's bread and cheese in the larder.'

'You're coming with me, my boy,' Nancy Field said firmly. 'It's an honour to get invited by a fine young lady like Rose Talbot, and I won't have you offending her by turning her down.'

Fortunately, the few items of clothing the cowboy possessed had been washed and ironed by his landlady during his illness. By the time they were due to call on Rose Talbot, Shand was looking quite presentable. The only thing that bothered Nancy Field was his refusal to go out without his Colt .45 at his hip. On this point he was adamant.

'I just wouldn't feel right without it,' he told her. 'Besides, it's Saturday night. What if we ran into trouble on the way?'

The door was opened to them by a middle-aged black maid, who noticed the gun at once and sniffed disapprovingly. Rose Talbot didn't even seem to see the gun as she came forward to greet them. She looked radiant in a blue dress that matched her eyes and showed off her slim figure to advantage. She seemed genuinely pleased that the young cowboy had been able to make it.

'Will you have a cold beer before we sit down to eat?' she asked him. 'I guess you must be thirsty after a day in the store.'

To her surprise he declined the offer, saying that he'd prefer a glass of cold water.

'I ain't that much of a drinker, Miss Talbot,' he explained, which was true. What he didn't say was that he was still feeling the effects of his exertions and was afraid that alcohol might make him fall asleep.

Over supper they talked about Mr Pritchard the hardware merchant, who'd kindly offered Paul Shand the job. Nancy Field had known Pritchard for years and she was glad to fill in the background to his life.

'Mr Pritchard had a son called Wallace,' she

said. 'That's Jamie's father, of course. Unlike
Jamie, Wallace never took an interest in the
family business. He was born with a roving spirit.
Well, one fine day when he was still only in his
teens Wallace informed the Pritchards that he'd
had enough of Larkwood and was going to seek
his fortune elsewhere. There was quite a scene
because he was their only child and they did their
best to dissuade him. When he went it broke his
mother's heart and she died a few years later.'

She stopped speaking as the maid came in
with fresh dishes.

'Mr Pritchard did get letters from Wallace once
in a while,' she resumed. 'He'd made it as far as
St Louis; that's where he got married and his son
Jamie was born. Then the war started and
Wallace was conscripted. I can remember how
worried his father was about him at the time, but
that went for lots of folk whose sons had gone
away, I suppose. Well, Wallace survived the war
and even got decorated for bravery. Then, when
Mr Pritchard thought his son might return at
last and bring his wife and child with him, he got
another letter to say that Wallace had been
gunned down in an alleyway in St Louis. It was
his widow who wrote the letter, and that wasn't
all the bad news she had for him. She said she'd
picked up with a riverboat gambler who wanted
nothing to do with her child. I remember Mr

Pritchard setting out for St Louis to fetch the boy home; otherwise it would have been the orphanage for Jamie Pritchard.'

'It's a tragic story, but at least it had a happy ending,' Rose Talbot commented, and Paul Shand nodded in agreement.

'Well, I hope that's how Jamie Pritchard sees it,' Nancy Field said ominously. 'Sometimes I think his grandfather is far too strict on him. I hope Mr Pritchard doesn't push him too far, or Jamie may decide to break out just like his father did. . . .'

Over at the Frontiersman saloon the bar-room was packed with hard-drinking and hard-gambling cowboys and miners. On busy nights the regular bartender was allowed to hire extra help to cope with the crowds. Tonight he was concerned about the number of customers who'd failed to hand their guns over the bar. It was a rule in every saloon in Larkwood and normally Con Meadows saw that it was respected in the Frontiersman, but where was he?

Eventually the bartender decided to go and see the saloon owner, Wilson Emery, in his private office and appraise him of the situation.

He found the lawyer and Con Meadows engaged in deep conversation over a bottle of bourbon. Emery heard the bartender out, but didn't take the usual step of sending the gunslinger Meadows to handle things.

'Get word to the marshal,' he ordered curtly. 'If he's got time to waste patrolling the Talbot bank, he can see to law and order in Larkwood for a change.'

After their evening was over at Rose Talbot's house Paul Shand accompanied Nancy Field back to the boarding-house. Hearing the din coming from the drinking dens and seeing the number of drunks on the sidewalk, the landlady was not sorry that her young lodger had insisted on wearing his gunbelt.

Then a stocky figure emerged from the shadows and almost collided with them. When she saw the tin star glistening on his shirt-front she realized that it was Powell the town marshal and she sighed with relief. The lawman tilted the rim of his Stetson and muttered a word of apology, but his mind seemed fixed on other matters.

'It's all right, Marshal,' she assured him. 'I wasn't looking where I was going. I don't envy you your job tonight, not with all this riff-raff out on the streets.'

'It's the riff-raff that's still inside that worries me, Nancy,' he replied. 'Seems some fellers in Emery's place won't hand their guns in. I'm on my way there now.'

The pale light from the saloons showed up the deep furrows on his forehead. He was no longer a young man.

'You're not going there alone, are you?' she

enquired anxiously. 'Can't you get any help?'

'Nope,' he said. 'Though I'll need some soon. This township's getting too boisterous for one man to manage.'

With a brief nod to Nancy Field's companion the lawman was on his way to the Frontiersman. It was this show of independence that made Paul Shand's mind up.

'Hold on a minute, Marshal,' he said. 'Let's both of us walk Mrs Field home; then I'll go with you to the saloon.'

Powell hesitated a moment and Nancy Field decided not to interfere. She didn't want her young lodger risking his life, but on the other hand the marshal was a good man who deserved support.

'OK,' Powell said almost reluctantly. 'Only you let me do the talking, understood?'

The young cowboy was quite prepared to defer to the lawman's experience and authority.

'I understand, Marshal,' he said. 'You can do the talking.'

When they walked through the swing-doors of the Frontiersman saloon hardly any of the customers paid them any attention. Powell had to shout at the top of his voice to still the hubbub.

'Those of you toting guns better hand them in right now,' he yelled. 'You know the law round here.'

Most of the men seemed genuinely surprised to find that they were still armed. Normally Con Meadows dispossessed them of their guns when they entered the saloon. Good-humouredly they trooped to the counter with their gunbelts. But one well-built young miner persisted in wearing his .45 despite the lawman's warning.

'I mean you too, young feller,' Powell told him.

The youngster glanced at the group of friends around him and then grinned mischievously.

'I'm only gonna be here a few minutes, old-timer,' he said. 'Ain't no point in me handing in my gun.'

Powell extended his left hand but the young miner didn't budge. As Paul Shand moved level with the marshal one of the other miners gave him a word of warning.

'Careful what you're doing, kid,' he said. 'Moose is good.'

'I know he is,' Shand replied in a voice that made the spectators fall silent. 'If he'll go up against a stranger he must be good, or a fool and he don't look much like a fool to me.'

The only noise now was the shuffling of men trying to get out of the line of fire. Moose and Paul Shand stood there staring into each other's eyes for a while, then a nervous smile played on the young miner's lips.

'You called my bluff, cowboy,' he said, moving

his hand well clear of the handle of his Colt. 'I ain't no gunfighter; the marshal can have my gun any time he likes.'

Powell didn't wait for him to change his mind. He stepped forward and removed the six-shooter from its holster. Then he turned and addressed the man who'd spoken to Paul Shand a few moments earlier.

'You're a bad friend, mister,' he admonished him. 'Your big mouth almost caused a shooting just now.'

The man blushed bright scarlet and turned away. None of the company followed him.

'I'm going to talk to Wilson Emery,' Powell told Shand. 'I need to put him straight on a few things. Then I'm gonna take you over to the Red Stag and buy you a drink.'

Despite his misgivings Shand didn't want to upset the lawman by turning the offer down.

'Okay,' he agreed. 'I'll wait for you in the street.'

As the young cowboy stood on the saloon steps, the doors swung open and the shadow of a man appeared on the sidewalk and stayed motionless. Shand hoped there was no more trouble on the way.

'Don't worry, it's only me,' Brad Mantle told him. 'I couldn't help you in there because I'd handed my gun in. Anyway, you handled it pretty well.'

Paul Shand turned to face him. In one way it was nice to see Mantle; in another it wasn't.

'Thanks,' he said. 'How are you doing?'

Mantle told him briefly about his new job on the ranch; he'd come into Larkwood tonight at the invitation of some of the ranch hands. For his part Shand remembered to thank Mantle for paying all the bills he'd incurred during his sickness.

'You're thanking the wrong person,' Mantle said. 'I didn't pay a cent. I offered to, but it was all taken care of.'

Shand lapsed into a thoughtful silence, so Mantle asked him if he'd seen or heard anything of Parsons and the others.

'Nope,' Shand replied. 'I don't particularly want to. Do you?'

Brad Mantle merely shrugged his shoulders and walked back into the saloon, leaving the question unanswered.

TEN

Nancy Field had another surprise for her young lodger when she returned from church the next morning. She'd been talking to Rose Talbot again, and Rose had offered to take Paul Shand out for a ride that afternoon in her gig.

'A few hours in the fresh air will do you good,' the landlady advised him. 'So don't go eating too much at midday, because Rose told me she's preparing a picnic for the two of you. She reckons you need building up after your illness.'

When Rose turned up in the gig in the early afternoon, she was less formally dressed than the previous evening. She had on a grey cotton blouse and a brown skirt, and she still looked wonderful.

'Do you mind if I drive?' she asked him as he climbed up by her side. 'The grey is my favourite horse and I haven't had a chance to drive it all week.'

He didn't mind; it was just nice to be with her. She chose a wide, even trail out of town, because the gig never was the most stable of vehicles. They drove for five or six miles before coming to a stop by the side of a brook where there were some trees to give them shade. Shand untied the picnic hamper at the rear of the gig and placed it on the grassy bank. Rose opened it and took out a pink linen tablecloth, which she laid out on the ground by the side of them. She looked very happy as she set out the picnic on the cloth, with the young cowboy looking on.

'I know you're not a drinker, Paul,' she said, 'but my uncle left me quite a store of wine. I think he'd like me to share some of it with my friends.'

He tasted it, and found it pleasantly sweet and warming.

'Is it all right?' she asked as she distributed the sandwiches.

'It tastes fine,' he assured her, and quietly compared the redness of the wine to the colour of his companion's lips.

She realized he was staring at her and she averted her gaze, but she knew that he liked what he saw, and her bosom swelled as she took in extra air.

'Red wine will help build you up,' she said. 'But be careful; wine of this quality is strong. I don't suppose you're . . .'

Her voice trailed off. The last thing she wanted to do was offend her guest. Paul Shand read her mind and hastened to reassure her.

'I guess I ain't much of a wine drinker at all,' he admitted cheerfully. 'And especially not the sort that's served out of a fancy bottle like this.'

They both fell silent, aware that their circumstances were quite different. Rose Talbot was obviously wealthy, whereas Paul was still surviving from day to day. But even more important was the fact that they liked each other's company. As they sat there, almost touching, Paul Shand realized that he needed to kiss her on the lips, even at the risk of breaking the spell. He needn't have worried; when their lips met, the spell became a rapture. Rose gave a little sigh and relaxed back on to the grass, allowing him to kiss her on the forehead, the cheeks, the eyes and the mouth.

'I hope you know what's happening, Paul,' she murmured. 'Because I'm not sure that I do.'

They hadn't been lying there long when a shot rang out nearby and made the cowboy jump to his feet.

'Be careful, Paul,' she urged him. 'It's nothing to do with us.'

But Shand was already running up the slope to gain height and get a better view of their surroundings.

He was relieved to find that there was nothing sinister going on. About a hundred yards away along the banks of the stream Jamie Pritchard and his friend, Floyd Toomes, the recently-appointed trainee cashier in the Talbot bank, were engaged in a bit of shooting practice, quite oblivious to the love scene they'd just interrupted. When Paul Shand told Rose Talbot what the two youngsters were up to she laughed with relief and suggested they take over the remains of the picnic for the boys to finish off.

Floyd Toomes was particularly impressed by his first meeting with Paul Shand. News of the way the young cowboy had backed up Marshal Powell in the Frontiersman saloon had spread like wildfire throughout the township. Jamie, too, was anxious to hear Shand's own account of the confrontation in the saloon, but Shand was too modest to elaborate on the role he'd played.

'It was the marshal's problem,' he said, 'and it was the marshal who solved it. I went along to help out, but I wasn't needed.'

Rose Talbot had heard otherwise outside church that morning. It had taken courage and tact to do what Shand had done the previous evening, yet here he was playing it all down. It made the girl feel very proud, and very much in love.

Jamie and Floyd were unconvinced by his

statement and they were eager to show him the skills they were acquiring by the secret practice they were putting in at a safe distance from Larkwood.

'We set stones up on the larger rocks and use them as targets,' Floyd explained. 'We compete with each other and that improves our concentration.'

They gave a brief demonstration and waited for the cowboy's reaction. When it came, it wasn't what they expected.

'It must be costing you boys a fortune in slugs,' he commented drily.

'Sure it does,' Jamie agreed. 'But we reckon it's worth it if we become crack shots.'

Floyd Toomes had detected a note of criticism in Shand's voice and he waited for the cowboy to explain.

'You need to be practising your draw,' Shand told them. 'What's the good in being a crack shot if the other feller gets a shot in first? Even if he only wings you you may not be in much shape to carry on fighting.'

The two of them digested his statement slowly. It made sense.

'Show us your draw, Paul,' Floyd asked him. 'Just to see if we're anywhere close to you.'

They both sucked in breath as he gave them a demonstration: he was swift and smooth.

'Is that your very fastest?' Jamie Pritchard enquired, and Paul Shand smiled.

'Nope,' he assured the lad. 'When I'm scared I can draw a lot faster than that.'

'It was all kind of a blur to me,' Floyd admitted. 'Can you show us how it's done? Just to put us on the right lines, I mean.'

Shand turned to Rose Talbot and she smiled and nodded her head. After all, Floyd was working for her now and he might need gun skills one day. And as for Jamie Pritchard, well, Jamie was Jamie and he'd do his own thing whatever obstacles he found in the way.

It took Paul Shand less than twenty minutes to make a marked improvement in the youngsters' gun-handling skills.

'You can practise yourselves from now on,' he told them. 'You've got the idea, so you can only get better. Just remember this one thing, though: however good you are in practice, the real thing can be very different. I've seen good men freeze and be killed by bums. Avoid trouble if you can, 'cause you can never be sure how it's going to end.'

It was almost evening before Rose Talbot and Paul Shand were back in the vicinity of Larkwood. As they approached the township the girl asked a favour of her companion.

'Do you mind if we call at the cemetery before

I drop you off?' she asked. 'I'd like to spend a few moments at my uncle's grave.'

Shand didn't mind one bit; the longer he spent in the girl's company the more he liked it. The shadows were lengthening as Rose halted the gig at the foot of the hillock where the town's dead were buried. They climbed a short distance to a fresh grave that was still festooned with wreaths and flowers.

'There was an attempted robbery at the bank a few days before you were brought in,' the girl explained. 'Uncle Julian got caught up in it and he was trampled by a horse.'

She was surprised by the way the colour drained from Paul Shand's face. For his part, he couldn't imagine why Mantle hadn't told him about the fatality. Nancy Field hadn't mentioned it either, probably thinking that it would be better if Rose told him herself.'

'Are you all right?' the girl enquired anxiously. 'You're still weak after all you've been through. Let's get you home.'

They walked back down the hill towards the gig. The buildings of the town looked almost black against the setting sun, just like Paul Shand's frame of mind . . .

Next morning in the hardware store Jamie Pritchard couldn't stop whistling to show how contented he was with life. Whenever his path crossed Shand's Jamie gave a wink or a secretive smile. However, when his grandfather returned from his midday break over at the Red Stag saloon the atmosphere changed immediately. The old man made straight for the storeroom at the back, where Paul Shand was sweeping up the dust.

'I've just been talking to Mr Toomes from the bank,' he announced. 'He told me how you'd taken his son Floyd and my grandson Jamie out somewhere to teach them how to shoot.'

Shand's heart sank; the old man's voice was quivering with anger, and he didn't give the cowboy a chance to explain.

'After me warning you all about Jamie and firearms,' Pritchard went on, 'you took him straight out and taught him to become a killer. So that's the way you repay a favour. If it wasn't for Rose Talbot I'd fire you on the spot. That's where I'm going now, to see Rose, and when I get back maybe I'll fire you anyway.'

Neither of them had seen Jamie Pritchard come in from the main store.

'It wasn't Paul's fault, Pop,' he said. 'Floyd and me . . .'

His grandfather turned on him fiercely.

'You keep out of this, boy,' he shouted. 'It doesn't concern you. Get back to your work.'

Pritchard's eyes were flashing fire, but Jamie didn't budge an inch.

'It does concern me, Pop,' he retorted. 'If Paul goes, I go; and you'd better believe me!'

ELEVEN

Brad Mantle could justly claim to have made headway since he'd taken over as foreman on the Tres Encinas ranch. Jack Hobbs had been a weak leader and he'd shown favouritism towards the big cowpoke Miles and that had undermined the enthusiasm of the other hands. Since his humiliation by Mantle, Miles had turned over a new leaf; although he maintained a sullen silence when the new foreman was around, his work rate had improved and he was no longer a passenger. As a result the other men were more willing to work and the ranch was running more efficiently than it had for years.

On the reverse side of the coin the ranch hands still seemed to be living in the shadow of their counterparts on the Dickens ranch. Dickens's cattle still grazed on Tres Encinas land with impunity, and Mantle's cowhands still avoided contact with Jeff Dickens's men, and especially with the handful of gunslingers he employed in case of trouble.

And then there were the Thompson brothers, Max and Pete. They still ignored each other's existence, and it was impossible for Mantle to send them out as a pair on range patrols. They had to be kept apart, and with only five men working for him Mantle found it irritating to have to worry about such details.

One morning Mantle decided to take Max Thompson and the reformed cowhand Miles to relieve Pete Thompson and the veteran cowboy Jones, who'd been camped for a week near the boundary of Tres Encinas territory. Mantle didn't need to go along but he chose to in order to familiarize himself with the terrain.

As they rode Thompson and Miles conversed freely together, but as usual Miles showed no willingness to talk to Mantle, which made discourse between the three of them impossible. His stubbornness was starting to grate on the gunslinger, but Mantle was determined not to show it; he knew that any further confrontation between them would be more serious than the first and he wasn't going to let Miles's childish sulkiness provoke a showdown.

When they reached the camp Pete Thompson and Jones had made in the hills Max Thompson also fell silent. He didn't mind greeting Jones, but he was darned if he was going to say howdee to his brother Pete. So it was an uneasy reunion, with half those present not speaking to the other half. It had been a long, hot ride, and suddenly Brad Mantle had had enough.

'Max,' he said, 'Pete . . .'

The two brothers turned to face him. Pete was about to saddle up.

'I want you to shake hands,' Mantle told them. 'Before we all split up.'

Neither of them moved. Mantle turned to the veteran cowpoke Jones.

'I thought only womenfolk sulk,' the gunslinger said. 'Why d'you reckon these boys don't just settle their differences with their fists?'

Jones shrugged his shoulders but didn't say a word. Meanwhile the two brothers had flushed with anger.

'Because Sue Johns would never let us,' Max Thompson blurted out. 'She said she'd sack us if we fought each other. And she's the boss.'

Brad Mantle looked deliberately all around him.

'I don't see no boss here except me,' he told them. 'That's the way it should be on the range. But if you boys would rather sulk than fight, that's fine by me.'

His words sank in slowly, then Pete Thompson

unbuckled his gunbelt and let it fall to the ground.

'I'll fight the sonofabitch,' he said. 'That's if he ain't scared.'

He hardly had time to raise his guard before Max was upon him, arms flailing like windmills.

The fight must have lasted some twenty minutes, though nobody bothered to time it. When they weren't on their feet trading punches, they were rolling in the dust, clawing and kicking each other. It finally ended when Pete threw a lucky punch that caught his brother in the solar plexus. Max gasped and sank to the floor.

Pete stood there looking down at him through a veil of blood and sweat; they'd both been badly bruised and cut in the encounter. They both took some time to get their breath back, and in the meantime Pete had spat out a couple of teeth his brother had dislodged.

'You mangy coyote,' he said in disgust. 'You've gone and spoilt my good looks.'

Suddenly Max grinned up at him.

'Good looks?' he said. 'I don't ever recall having a good-looking brother, but you always could fight a bit.'

He held out his hand and Pete helped him to his feet. All the ill-feeling had drained from them. Brad Mantle hastened to take advantage of the situation.

'You boys had better get back to the ranch with Jones,' he said. 'I'll stay overnight with Miles. Tell Stewart to take over from me tomorrow.'

'What about Sue?' Max Thompson enquired. 'How are we gonna explain away all of these bruises?'

'Tell her the truth,' Mantle replied. 'Tell her what I said about being the boss on the range. I'll take all the blame.'

That night Mantle told Miles to take the first watch. As far as they knew there weren't any Indians in the area, but it was always wise to keep a look-out for mountain cats or other wild animals that might be prowling about. As it happened the night passed uneventfully, and when his watch was over Mantle wrapped his blanket around him and slept peacefully until he was roused by the sound and smell of bacon sizzling in the pan. There was coffee made, too, and he accepted the mug Miles offered him with a nod of gratitude. They ate in their usual silence for a while, but then Miles spoke.

'I don't know how you managed to sleep so well,' he said. 'Not after me threatening to kill you.'

When Brad Mantle failed to comment the big cowpoke pursued the subject regardless.

'I guess you reckon I ain't got the guts to do it,' he said.

'I think you got the guts,' Mantle replied at last. 'Most men will kill if you push them too far. It's just that I don't take you for a coward, Miles. I don't think you'd shoot anyone in the back, or while he's sleeping.'

The sulky expression left Miles's face, and he looked all the better for it.

'I guess you read me right,' he admitted. 'But you did get me riled the first time we met.'

'It was your old foreman Jack Hobbs who got you riled, Miles,' Mantle said. 'I'm told that he always treated you like someone special. When I treated you like I would any of the boys, you lost your cool. That's Hobbs's fault, not mine.'

'So to you I'm just as good as the rest of the cowpunchers?' Miles asked.

'Sure,' Mantle said with a little smile. 'Or just as bad, if you like it better.'

They were still waiting for Stewart to turn up when they spotted a cloud of dust less than a mile to the north.

'Let's go see what it is,' Mantle suggested, much to his companion's dismay.

'It's probably some of Jeff Dickens's boys,' Miles told him. 'They're best left alone.'

'You stay here, if you like,' Mantle said, without a trace of reproach in his voice. 'I'll go check them out.'

But when he rode off the big cowpoke was only

a few yards behind him. It soon became clear that Miles was right: three men were driving some steers away from Tres Encinas land. When they drew nearer Mantle recognized Jack Dobbs who'd formerly been Sue Johns's foreman; with Hobbs was an older cowhand and also a slight, arrogant-looking youngster whose leering expression spelt trouble. The small cavalcade halted as Mantle and his companion approached. Mantle was the first to speak.

'Do these animals belong to you?' he asked.

'Cain't you read a brand, mister?' Jack Hobbs said sarcastically, confident of support. 'JD stands for Jeff Dickens.'

'But they've been grazing on Tres Encinas range,' Mantle pointed out. 'Pay me a quarter for each steer's pasture and you can go on your way.'

'Sorry, mister,' Hobbs replied, with a sideways glance at the young gunslinger. 'We ain't carrying no money.'

'That's OK,' Mantle assured him. 'You go get the money and the cattle will wait here with us.'

Hobbs was thinking up a reply when the youngster urged his mount forward. Miles, meanwhile, sat frozen in the saddle, hoping nobody was paying any attention to him. Thinking he was dealing with a cowpuncher, the young gunslinger fixed Mantle with a stare that was meant to turn him to stone. After a moment or two Mantle lowered his gaze to the youngster's gunbelt. Thinking that he'd gained some ascendancy over his adversary, the youngster let his hand drop to his Colt.

The sudden shot scattered the mavericks in panic. Miles gazed in stunned silence as the gunslinger slid from his saddle with blood trickling from his lips. Mantle's face was expressionless as the watched the man's life ebb away on the brown earth. Then he turned to face Jack Hobbs again.

'Your pardner's just died for a couple of dollars,' he said. 'Go and ask your boss if he reckons it was worth it.'

Mantle and Miles rode back a few miles until they met up with Stewart, who was on his way to their old camp. Before leaving them, Mantle advised them to make a new camp at a safe distance from the border with the Dickens ranch. He also told them to high-tail it home if they saw any of Dickens's men on the trail in search of vengeance.

Jones was waiting for him at the corral to tell him that Sue Johns wanted him to report to the ranch house without delay. He got there just in time to see the old *señora* usher the children into another room to leave the two of them alone. Sue Johns was very angry and she didn't mince her words.

'You know that I won't have the men fighting amongst themselves,' she said. 'Why did you encourage them to half-kill one another? Are you crazy?'

'The Thompsons . . . why?' Mantle asked. 'Have they started fighting again?'

'Not yet,' she conceded. 'But there must be better ways of settling grudges.'

'Maybe,' he agreed. 'But they hadn't come up with one till yesterday. By the way, if you want to know how bad I really am, I killed a man today.'

When she realized he wasn't joking her face lost its colour and she sat down heavily in the nearest chair. He gave her a brief description of the event.

'Don't you realize what you've done?' she asked. 'You've started a range war.'

'Not if Dickens has any sense,' Mantle said. 'There ain't no justice in stealing your land like that.'

'Justice?' she said. 'What's the use of justice if my children are killed?'

'What life will they have if they grow up scared of Jeff Dickens?' Mantle asked. 'He's half living off you now. What's gonna happen when he decides to take over altogether?'

Before she could reply, he'd gone out and slammed the door behind him.

TWELVE

Clara Emery couldn't believe her good fortune: out of the blue her husband Wilson had informed her that he was going to visit one of the outlying ranches in the surrey and that he'd like her to go along. Of course, she'd jumped at the offer; Wilson was usually so preoccupied with his affairs, business and personal, that they hadn't been out together in a month of Sundays.

So here she was sitting alongside the man she adored, on her way to visit the Dickens spread, where Wilson had important matters to discuss. Despite her contentment she couldn't refrain from bringing up one of her pet subjects, even at the risk of angering her husband.

'How is Rose Talbot coping with her responsibilities at the bank?' she asked sweetly. 'It must be a headache for a young girl like that.'

She was fond of reminding Wilson of the age

difference between him and his latest fancy, but he didn't rise to the bait.

'Strangely enough,' he replied, 'that's one of the reasons I want to talk to Jeff Dickens. Since Rose has no interest in expanding the bank, I see room for a rival venture in Larkwood. I'm going to sound Jeff out and see if he'd consider moving his account to a new bank if one started up.'

Clara liked the sound of that; she'd much rather have her husband and the attractive young lady on opposite sides rather than working in partnership.

'Do you think Jeff will agree?' she asked hopefully.

'Well, the timing's good,' Wilson said. 'Jeff's pretty sore about the way things are in Larkwood nowadays. He was in town a few days ago complaining to the marshal that one of his men was gunned down by the new foreman Sue Johns hired to replace Jack Hobbs.'

It was the first Clara Emery had heard of the shooting.

'What's the marshal going to do?' she asked.

'The usual — nothing,' her husband said contemptuously. 'He told Jeff Dickens it sounded like a fair fight to him, and anyway it was outside town limits. The sooner I can get Con Meadows or someone like him elected town marshal, the better it'll be for everybody.'

'The new foreman at the Tres Encinas is the man who brought Paul Shand in to see Doc Gray after their fight with the Indians,' Clara commented. 'Shand's the young man who's turned Rose Talbot's head so badly.'

She glanced sideways and saw that her husband's expression had hardened. She'd have to tread carefully.

'I'm told it isn't Paul Shand's fault,' she went on casually. 'It seems Rose has been throwing herself at him. She's at the store where he works every day. Folk say she'll need a bigger house soon to fit in all the pots and pans she's buying from Mr Pritchard! And it seems that Shand doesn't give a fig for her; she's the one doing all the chasing. It's a shame to see a young girl lower herself like that.'

They rode along in silence for a while. As they approached a grove of evergreens a rider detached himself from the shadows. Something inside her told Clara Emery that all was not well.

'Careful, Wilson,' she warned the lawyer. 'There's a man riding towards us.'

Emery followed her gaze and smiled reassuringly.

'It's all right, dear,' he told her. 'It's only Con Meadows.'

'Oh,' she murmured with relief. She didn't like Con Meadows but at least he was someone they knew. Emery reined in the pair of horses and waited for the gunslinger to approach.

'Howdee, Con,' he greeted him. 'What brings you here?'

The newcomer brought his horse right alongside; then, in a swift movement, he drew his .45 and levelled it at his employer.

'I'll take your gun now, Wilson,' he said.

Clara looked on with stupefaction as her husband handed over his Colt. Then Meadows brought it crashing down on the side of the lawyer's head and sent him tumbling to the ground. Clara didn't even have the time to plead for mercy before the gunslinger turned and emptied three bullets into her breast.

The news of the second violent death in less than a month spread through Larkwood and the surrounding ranches like wildfire. The story was almost unbelievable: on the day of the murder Con Meadows had ridden on ahead to the Dickens ranch while Wilson and Clara Emery had taken a more leisurely journey in the surrey. Con had reached the ranch without mishap, but after two hours there was still no sign of the Emerys.

Meadows and Jeff Dickens, the story went, had concluded that the surrey must have lost a wheel or broken an axle, so Meadows had retraced his steps to give them a hand. When he arrived at the surrey he found the lawyer severely concussed and Clara Emery dead on the seat of the surrey, her dress soaked with blood.

Just about the whole town turned out for the funeral, since Clara was a more popular figure than her husband. Free drinks were available at the Frontiersman saloon after the burial, but Wilson Emery's grief was too great for him to be present. Instead he let it be known that he would be at home to receive visits from special friends. One of those special people was Rose Talbot and he was very much looking forward to receiving her expressions of sympathy.

Unfortunately, Rose chose to turn up accompanied by that store assistant, Paul Shand, who looked uncomfortable throughout the visit. Emery found the cowboy's presence irksome; he'd planned to break down in a controlled fashion and kindle some emotion in the girl's heart, but now none of that was possible, and he could feel his resentment against Shand growing by the minute.

Even less welcome was the visit by the town marshal. For some reason the lawman remained puzzled by the vicious slaying of Clara Emery. He'd refrained from questioning the lawyer too closely prior to the funeral but now, with a glass of Emery's best cognac in his hand, he expressed his concerns freely.

'It just doesn't make sense to me, Mr Emery,' he said between sips.

The lawyer took a deep breath before he spoke.

'I told you the story the day it happened,' he replied. 'I can't remember any more details.'

'You were still concussed when we spoke,' Powell reminded him. 'But you were pretty definite that you didn't recognize the killer.'

'That's right,' Emery agreed. 'He was right by us and I'd never seen him before.'

'So, he didn't try to hide his face – with a neckerchief, I mean?'

'Nope. That's why I didn't suspect anything was wrong. I let him draw up real close.'

'If he wasn't worried about being identified,' Powell remarked, 'he most likely knew he was going to kill you.'

'I guess so,' the lawyer said. 'As soon as I said we weren't carrying money, he only had killing on his mind.'

'But he didn't kill you,' Powell went on. 'And I cain't figure out why. And he used your gun to kill your wife, which is another puzzle.'

If he'd used his own gun it would still have been smelling when he reached the Dickens ranch, Emery thought to himself; that had been the masterstroke.

'I just don't know, Marshal,' he said. 'But what if you do catch him? Will you do what you did when Jeff Dickens's cowhand was gunned down by Sue Johns's new foreman – just let it ride?'

The lawman didn't rise to the bait. It was widely known that Jeff Dickens was hiring gunslingers to back up his aggressive plans for the ranch, but this wasn't the time to argue about it; not this soon after the funeral.

'You can be sure of one thing, Mr Emery,' he replied in an even tone of voice. 'I'll do what I think is right; that's how I've always acted.'

When the marshal had left, his last visitor was Con Meadows. Con wasn't there to offer his condolences but to seal a deal they'd struck a few days earlier. He didn't beat about the bush.

'If you've drawn up the contract,' he said bluntly, 'I want to read it.'

'Of course,' the lawyer replied. 'It's in the top drawer of the desk.'

Meadows walked across to the desk and retrieved a bulky envelope from the drawer. He removed the documents inside and eyed them critically.

'Looks pretty darned complicated to me,' he said querulously.

'That's because of the clauses we both agreed to,' Emery told him. 'Your share in the profits are confined to any new ventures we undertake together, not what I've accumulated in the past.'

'Not what you and your wife accumulated in the past,' Meadows reminded him caustically.

'Be that as it may,' Emery said, 'our deal starts from now, so it's in your interests to make the partnership work as well as it possibly can.'

The gunslinger glanced up at him; he found it easier to read the boss's mind than all that legal jargon. He could tell from the lawyer's tone of voice that he wanted something.

'Talk on,' he said.

'If that feller Paul Shand gets his feet under Rose Talbot's table, we'll never get our hands on the bank,' Emery said. 'Can you think of a way to get rid of him without any scandal?'

Meadows walked over to the window and stared out; he was deep in thought. Wilson Emery had touched on something that had been on his mind for weeks. He could remember Brad Mantle serving in the same army unit as Captain Parsons during the war. Mantle had claimed to be prospecting in the hills at the time of the raid on the Larkwood bank, and Paul Shand was there with him. Did that mean that there was a connection between the cowboy Shand and Captain Parsons' outlaw band?

That night, after completing his last patrol before hitting the hay, Marshal Alvin Powell found that someone had slipped a note under the jailhouse door. When he read it he realized that he had another problem on his hands.

THIRTEEN

Paul Shand was rudely awakened when the curtain was pulled sharply across the window of his room to let in the dawn light from the east. He reached instinctively for the gunbelt draped over the headrest of the bed, but it wasn't where he'd left it.

'Take it easy,' a voice said. 'You and me need to talk.'

The cowboy blinked a couple of times to adjust to the sunlight. Town Marshal Alvin Powell was sitting next to the window, with Shand's gunbelt in an untidy heap at his feet. The lawman had a piece of paper in his hand and he proceeded to read it in a voice that was soft but nonetheless perfectly audible. When he finished the recitation he waited for the young cowboy's reaction.

For his part Paul Shand was experiencing a mixture of emotions: unease about the punish-

ment the law might mete out to him, and relief
that the lie he'd been living was at last exposed.

'I was a member of the gang that attacked the
bank,' he admitted, 'but I didn't take part in the
raid. I'd only just joined them and they didn't
know how far they could trust me. I waited for
them at our camp, but they never got back. I
haven't seen hair nor hide of them since, and I
don't want to.'

The marshal was studying his face for any hint
of a lie.

'There may be other notes like this one for
folks to read,' he said. 'I guess you know what
that means.'

'Sure; you're taking me in.'

'Nope,' Powell replied. 'I reckon I owe you for
your support the other night. I believe what
you've told me, but you cain't stay on in town. You
and Larkwood are finished for good.'

Paul Shand couldn't believe he was getting off
so lightly. His mind turned to another matter.

'Will you speak to Rose Talbot, Marshal?' he
said. 'If she knows what I've been keeping from
her, it may explain the strange way I've been
acting. Tell her. . . tell her I never wanted to hurt
her.'

'I'll do that,' the lawman promised. 'By the way,
that Mantle feller who brought you into town. Is
he part of the gang?'

When Shand didn't answer the marshal clicked his tongue sadly.

'Mantle's already killed one man since he's been working for Sue Johns,' he said. Looks like she's landed herself in a heap of trouble. And as for you, young feller, you've got fifteen minutes to get out of town!'

When the big cowpoke Miles got back to the Tres Encinas ranch after escorting Sue Johns to and from Clara Emery's funeral in Larkwood, he had bad news for his fellow cowpunchers.

'I met Jack Hobbs in town,' he told them. 'Seems Jeff Dickens is hopping mad about what Mantle did to his hired gun. He's swearing vengeance. When the time is right him and his boys are gonna come here and string Mantle up – and any of us who tries to stop them.'

The young cowhand Max Thompson and the veteran Stewart were there in the bunkhouse listening to him relate the tale.

'Dickens has got at least two other gunslingers on the payroll,' Max remarked. 'And he's got half a dozen cowhands, counting Hobbs. We wouldn't stand a chance against odds like that. What do you think, Stewart?'

The older man was thoughtfully chewing a twist of tobacco.

'If you live as long as I have,' he commented

drily, 'you'll learn that the odds cain't be with you every time.'

Miles couldn't forget how scared he'd been when Mantle had faced up to Jeff Dickens's gunslinger.

'If we go up against the Dickens outfit, I ain't gonna get to live that long anyways,' he said.

'Let's wait and see what happens,' Stewart advised. 'Me, I'll probably face it out. I ain't really got any place else to go.'

Miles almost jumped out of his skin when the stranger appeared at the barn door and asked for Brad Mantle. Max Thompson was supposed to be keeping look-out in case Jeff Dickens and his men came a-visiting. What if this man was a hired gun come to settle accounts with the Tres Encinas foreman? Before he could reply to the question Brad Mantle was already crossing the yard to see what was up. To the big cowpoke's relief, Mantle and the stranger greeted one another cordially and then walked off in the direction of the corral, deep in conversation.

From the window of the house Sue Johns had also noted the man's arrival. When Brad Mantle came into the ranch house a few minutes later she could tell that something serious had happened.

'What's wrong, Brad?' she asked. 'What does that feller want?'

It was much worse than she was expecting.

'I'm quitting,' he told her bluntly. 'I've got to leave.'

Despite all their disagreements, her stomach churned over at his words. In a short space of time he'd become part of the ranch, part of her life. The colour drained from her face.

'What do you mean, you're quitting?' she said. 'You can't just quit.'

'That youngster out there is called Paul Shand,' Mantle said. 'He's the one I said was prospecting with me in the hills.'

'I know all that,' Sue replied. 'Since then he's made quite an impression on Rose Talbot, who owns the bank in Larkwood.'

'That's the problem,' Mantle said grimly. 'Someone's spread the word that him and me were mixed up in the bank raid a few weeks ago. Shand's been run out of town, and I could be next.'

Sue Johns listened to him in disbelief.

'So you were there when Julian Talbot got killed?' she asked.

'Nope; Shand and me weren't nowhere near the town even. But the fellers that were are friends of mine. I cain't tell you how sorry I am, Sue.'

For a few moments she looked helpless and dejected, but when he turned towards the door she moved swiftly to block his path.

'You're not going,' she told him. 'The townsfolk can think what they like, and so can the marshal. When my husband was killed I got no help from Larkwood – no help at all till you came along. If you'd been involved in the bank raid it would be different, I'd go tell Powell myself, about both of you.'

Her defiance made her look even more beautiful, but still Mantle shook his head.

'I cain't leave Paul Shand in the lurch,' he said. 'I'm the one who brought him into the gang. He's had nothing but bad luck ever since.'

'You don't need to,' Sue told him. 'There's a dugout in the hills where the cowhands shelter in bad weather. It's got a view for miles around. I'll take him there, Brad. We'll keep him supplied with food. It'll give you time, Brad – time to think.'

Mantle was thinking already. She was right. Where did they have to run to? Then he snapped out of his reverie and smiled suddenly.

'You're one helluva lady, Sue Johns,' he told her. 'One helluva lady!'

FOURTEEN

When Captain Parsons decided the time was ripe for his depleted band of outlaws to return to Larkwood, little did he foresee the violence he was about to stir up. But return he must, if only to ascertain what had become of Brad Mantle and Paul Shand and the money the gang had accumulated in previous robberies.

He had little fear of being recognized since the ill-fated bank raid had been over in a flash. Dixon's injured hand had healed quickly and was no longer bandaged. As usual, Parsons himself went into town to reconnoitre; his first port of call was the Frontiersman saloon where he met up with Con Meadows, who had to think quickly to answer the outlaw leader's questions.

'Mantle and Shand were both in town for a while,' Con Meadows informed him. 'Since then Mantle has been working as ranch foreman for a widow called Sue Johns. Shand was in town longer; he'd got wounded in a fight with some Indians and he was pretty sick for a while. A few days ago word got about that Shand was involved in the bank raid that killed Julian Talbot. The marshal ran him out of town.'

Parsons looked at him suspiciously.

'What do you mean, word got about?' he said. 'How did word get about?'

'He had a fever when Mantle brought him into Larkwood,' Meadows said, hoping he sounded convincing. 'He must have let something slip.'

'Is Mantle still at the ranch?'

'I don't know,' Meadows replied, truthfully this time. 'I can always find out for you.'

'Yeah,' Parsons said. 'In the meantime, we need money and somewhere to stay. What about this place, Con?'

Meadows was thinking quickly; only recently his boss Wilson Emery had been talking of taking on extra men to increase his prestige in the township.

'I'll see what I can do,' he replied defensively. 'In the meantime I think we better keep quiet about knowing each other.'

'You're right,' Parsons commented with a wry smile. 'You always were discreet, Con.'

In the event things worked out pretty smoothly. Within a couple of hours of being in town, the gang had caught the attention of Emery himself.

'D'you know them, Con?' he asked his partner.

'I met one of them this morning,' Meadows said. 'He looks quite useful. I don't know the others.'

'Talk to them,' Emery told him. 'If you think they'll do, hire them. They can share the empty room upstairs.'

But Emery was only divulging half his plans to his partner. The next morning Parsons came and sat next to Con Meadows, who was reading the local gazette near the front window of the saloon.

'The saloon-owner, Wilson, is a fine feller,' he said, rubbing his forehead. 'He must have treated me to two bottles last night.'

Before Meadows could comment, the gang leader lowered his voice.

'What do you have on him, Con?' he asked.

Meadows looked at him in astonishment.

'What d'you mean?' he said.

'I mean, what do you have on him that makes him offer a thousand dollars to see you dead. . . ?'

It was way after dark when the bartender of the Frontiersman saloon saw Parsons walk through the swing doors of the bar. Parsons, Meadows and the other members of the gang had left town in the late afternoon, looking like they were on some kind of mission. But now Parsons was alone.

'Is Mr Emery here or at home?' he asked the barman.

'Upstairs,' the man informed him. 'Since Clara got killed he don't go home.'

Wilson Emery heard his footsteps on the staircase and went out into the passageway to meet him.

'Well, is he dead?' he enquired, with a note of anxiety in his voice.

'Not yet, Mr Emery,' Parsons replied. 'There's been a hitch.'

'Hitch . . . what do you mean, a hitch?'

'I guess I misjudged my men,' Parsons said. 'Things have been going so bad for us lately, they wouldn't kill Meadows just on my say-so. They want to hear it from you. That way they reckon you won't be able to turn them in later.'

The annoyance showed in the lawyer's face. Was Parsons running an organized gang or a rabble of ruffians?

'Hold on a minute,' Emery said. 'I'll go fetch my coat.'

They joined up with the rest of the outlaws about a mile out of town. The gang had found a suitable tree from which to hang Meadows, who already had his hands tied behind his back. Formally, the lawyer repeated his orders to

Mitch, Fenton and Dixon. Still they looked uncertain.

'They need it in writing, Mr Emery,' Parsons explained. 'I got a piece of paper all ready for you to say how you killed your wife, too.'

'But that's preposterous,' Emery exclaimed. 'I'll never write that!'

Then Mitch took one step forward and slapped him hard across the face.

'Then we'll have to beat it out of you, Mr Emery,' he told him.

The third death in succession among Larkwood's leading citizens was also the most macabre. Wilson Emery's body was dumped unceremoniously outside the jailhouse door at dead of night, to be found by Marshal Alvin Powell the next morning.

The lawyer's neck bore the marks of hanging or garrotting, and he'd been badly beaten before he died. A handwritten note in his jacket pocket bore witness that he had murdered his wife, and it was that note which took the wind out of the marshal's sails. Although he and the rest of the townsfolk cast suspicious glances in the direction of the gang now occupying the Frontiersman saloon, there was no clamour for justice or revenge. Nobody felt any sympathy for a self-confessed wife-slayer who'd always been an arrogant sonofabitch.

Powell went through the motions of calling at the saloon and talking to Meadows and the others, but he was met by a wall of silence. However, Con Meadows did deign to show him the contract Emery had signed, which made him the saloon owner's business partner.

'I guess that makes me the owner of the Frontiersman, Marshal,' the gunslinger informed the lawman cheerfully. 'The law firm I cain't handle. I'll make do with what I got here.'

Powell didn't press the matter; he was outnumbered by this grinning bunch of newcomers to town. He knew they were behind Emery's death, but he had no proof. All he could do was retire to the jailhouse and brood over the odd situation prevailing in Larkwood.

Despite his apparent stroke of luck, Con Meadows had plenty on his mind as well. He was stuck with a dangerous band of outlaws on his premises and he was in debt to them for his life. Captain Parsons had put loyalty before gain; what would he be asking in return? He found out that very evening.

'Tomorrow you'll bring Brad Mantle into town,' Parsons ordered. 'Tell him I'm looking for Paul Shand as well.'

It took only a matter of hours for the news of

Wilson Emery's demise to reach the outlying ranches. Sue Johns heard it from the big cowpoke Miles, who'd been told the story by a passing wagon-driver.

'Does Brad Mantle know?' she asked him. She hadn't seen Mantle since morning.

'I told him as soon as I got back,' Miles said. 'That's when Mantle rode off.'

She felt a sinking feeling in the pit of her stomach. Whenever there was bad news she feared it might be connected with the gunslinger's past. She didn't relax until Mantle returned to the ranch towards dusk.

'I've been to see Shand,' he said in reply to her question. 'I had to tell him about Emery. I reckon our old gang's mixed up in it. Tomorrow me and Shand are going into town.'

'You're leaving the ranch for good?' she asked fearfully.

He laid both his hands on her shoulders.

'Not before I've settled this business with Jeff Dickens,' he promised.

'It's not good enough, Brad,' she said. 'I don't want you to go away.'

'Me and Parsons go back a long way,' he told her, his face lined and troubled. Suddenly she was pressed against him and their lips met in a fierce embrace.

'Let's not waste tonight,' she urged him.

'Tomorrow you're a free man. . . .'

When Mantle awoke early the next morning she was no longer by his side. He could hear her moving about in the kitchen, preparing his breakfast. As he ate it she watched him in silence, and then he was gone. As it happened, his journey to the hideout was a waste of time. Paul Shand had already left for town.

FIFTEEN

It was still dark when Marshal Alvin Powell heard a muffled knock on the back door of the jailhouse. He'd been sleeping fully dressed because he was expecting trouble to break out at any time. His Colt .45 was in his hand when he opened the door.

'Shand,' he said, the surprise showing in his voice. 'What brings you to Larkwood?'

The young cowboy slipped past him and into the jailhouse; he was still covered by the wary lawman's Colt.

'Brad Mantle told me you've got strangers in town,' Paul Shand explained. 'They are the gang who raided your bank, and I reckon they may try again. I'm scared for Rose Talbot.'

'What are you going to do about it?' Powell enquired.

'I don't know,' the cowboy admitted. 'I was hoping you had some ideas.'

The marshal sheathed his six-gun and sat down wearily in his chair.

'Will you testify about their part in the bank raid?' he asked and Paul Shand nodded his head. 'In that case I've gotta reason to arrest them, though God knows where I'll get the fire-power from to do it. Can I swear you in as a deputy?'

'Sure,' Paul Shand told him, 'if you're willing to take an ex-outlaw.'

'Right now I'll take anyone I can get, Paul,' the lawman sighed. 'Let's swear you in. It's a start at least.'

By the time Con Meadows had got within a mile of the Tres Encinas ranch, Brad Mantle was on his way to town by an alternative route, having failed to rendezvous with Paul Shand at the hide-out. What Meadows did glimpse was a group of almost a dozen riders also headed for the ranch house. He was hidden from their view by the glare of the sun that was still quite low on the eastern horizon. He was close enough to them to recognize Jeff Dickens and Jack Hobbs and their motley crowd of gunslingers and ordinary cowpokes.

Meadows had no doubt that they, too, were

looking for Brad Mantle, not to take him back to town but to kill him as Jeff Dickens had sworn to do. Dickens had had no satisfaction from the marshal in Larkwood so now he was going to mete out his own form of justice. Meadows saw no point in going on; he turned his horse round and headed straight back to town.

When the horsemen reached the ranch buildings it was the *señora* who raised the alarm.

'Susanna,' she called out in Spanish. 'The corral is full of men. Keep the children inside.'

When the door of the ranch house opened, Jeff Dickens was disappointed to see Sue Johns standing there, rather than the man he was after.

'Where's Mantle hiding?' he demanded. 'Tell him to come and face me.'

The young woman glanced round the yard. None of her cowhands was in sight. She couldn't blame them for running away from these odds.

'Brad isn't here,' she said, struggling to keep her voice steady. 'I don't know where he is.'

'He's there all right,' Dickens snarled. 'He's got two minutes to come out, or we start burning the place down. You've already lost one husband,' he added callously. 'So you know I mean business.'

Whitefaced and trembling, Sue Johns turned and went back inside the house. The door had hardly closed behind her when the shooting started.

*

Marshal Alvin Powell did his morning rounds as usual, but his new deputy didn't leave the jailhouse. The handful of people who called at the jail didn't react to Shand's presence; after recent events it would have taken an earthquake to move them. Towards midday the lawman returned with a written message for Paul Shand from Rose Talbot.

'I've been beside myself with worry since you left, Paul,' it read. 'The marshal thinks you're a good person and I know that he's right. I need to talk to you. Please don't deny me that chance.'

As he read it Powell was watching a horseman dismount outside the Frontiersman saloon further along the high street.

'Isn't that Mantle?' the marshal asked. 'Come and take a look.'

Shand crossed to the window and confirmed Powell's suspicions.

'That's made the odds even worse,' the lawman commented grimly. 'If they intend to hit the bank it could happen any time now.'

'Did you have any luck signing up deputies?' Shand asked.

'I had two volunteers,' Powell said ruefully: 'Jamie Pritchard and Floyd Toomes. I turned them both down – they're just kids.'

Meanwhile, Brad Mantle was not enjoying his

reunion with his outlaw friends in the bar of the Frontiersman.

'Con Meadows has been looking for you everywhere,' Captain Parsons greeted him. 'He got back half an hour ago. Do you know where Shand is?'

When Mantle shook his head Mitch was happy to bring him up to date.

'He's over at the jailhouse, wearing a deputy's star,' the gunslinger told him. 'I bet he's told the marshal everything about us.'

'I want you and Shand back with the rest of us,' Parsons said quietly. 'I don't want no feuding between us.'

'That's not going to be easy for me, Captain,' Mantle pointed out. 'Not right away. I got unfinished business out on the ranch where I'm working.'

'Your unfinished business is showing us where you left our money,' the gang leader snapped. 'But first you'll go over to the jailhouse and bring your friend Shand back here. That's an order.'

Alvin Powell watched Mantle like a hawk as he approached the jailhouse. Paul Shand opened the door to the gunslinger while the marshal kept him covered with his .45. When Mantle had relayed the captain's instructions, Shand's reply was curt.

'Tell him I only take orders from the marshal here,' he said.

As the gunslinger turned to leave, Powell addressed him suddenly.

'Whose side are you on in all this, Mantle?' he asked.

'Nobody's,' Mantle replied. 'I got problems of my own.'

Dixon was standing inside the doorway of the Frontiersman saloon, rifle in hand. He watched Mantle retrace his steps across the road.

'There's no sign of Shand,' he informed the others, as if they couldn't see that far. 'Mantle's by himself.'

Parson's face was set like stone and a blue vein was throbbing in his forehead. Larkwood had already cost him one man dead, and now his gang was in danger of breaking up.

'Bring him down, but don't aim to kill,' he ordered. 'He knows where the money is.'

Dixon fired once and Brad Mantle crumpled over on to his side in the dusty road, with a bullet in his left thigh. Dixon waited for a few moments before venturing out into the street. He'd walked half-way towards the inert body when suddenly Mantle's free arm jerked into life and his six-gun glinted in the sun. Mantle fired twice in quick succession and Dixon took the full impact of both shots. He hit the ground with a dull thud and blood trickled from his mouth on to the brown earth. Then Marshal Powell opened fire on the windows of the saloon with his Winchester repeater in an attempt to give Brad Mantle some cover.

The next few minutes were frustrating for Paul Shand because the only signs of the enemy were the puffs of smoke from their rifles and six-shooters. Mantle, meanwhile, either wouldn't or couldn't move from where he lay.

'They ain't gonna venture out the front way,' Powell said suddenly, 'but there's a staircase at the back of the saloon. They may use it to outflank us.'

'I'll go round there,' Shand told him. 'I'll head them off.'

'Well, go out the back way,' Powell said. 'And don't take any risks. We're outnumbered as it is.'

He heard the back door of the jail close as Shand set off, but all the lawman's attention was fixed on the saloon on the opposite side of the street. He could see no hope of Mantle surviving as things were. Then the unexpected happened: a handcart piled with boxes and metal utensils creaked its way across the road towards where the stricken gunslinger lay. It was being propelled from behind by the two youngsters he'd earlier turned down as deputies.

Despite the hostile fire emanating from the Frontiersman which ricocheted off the pots and pans and shot splinters out of the wooden containers, the two lads persisted until they'd pushed the cart to a point where Mantle was completely shielded. Then Jamie and Floyd lay flat out on the earth underneath the cart and proceeded to take pot-shots at the outlaws lurking in the saloon. They had acted just in time; Captain Parsons and his henchman Mitch had at last thought of going to the upstairs windows to get a better view of the street and the prostrate Mantle, and now they were frustrated and angered by the new turn of events.

Paul Shand moved in a wide arc to get to the other side of the street and behind the Frontiersman saloon. On his way he noticed with relief the cart standing in the middle of the road, but he had no idea who had managed to move it there. Mantle was sitting up now, leaning against the vehicle, so he obviously hadn't been harmed further.

Shand reached a point from where he could observe the steps leading to the upper floor of the saloon. The firing round the front was only sporadic now as if everybody was taking a breather. He was itching to climb those steps but he knew it would be foolhardy; somebody could be waiting inside with a shotgun to blow him in half. No, Parsons was the one who was trapped; let him make the first move.

Back in the jailhouse the marshal was feeling

more relaxed, too. The situation out front was stable for the moment and he had confidence that his new deputy wouldn't do anything reckless and jeopardize their safety. Then the back door of the jail swung open and Jack Hobbs and two other men walked into the room.

'Stop firing – stop firing!'

Jamie Pritchard turned his head in the direction of the shouting. A small group of men had come out of the jail and were crossing the road. Marshal Powell was the one doing the shouting and Jack Hobbs was the man holding the Colt against the side of the lawman's head. Two Stetsonned cowboys were following them closely.

'Drop your guns,' Hobbs ordered the youngsters crouched behind the cart, and they complied reluctantly. Mantle's gun was already lowered; He'd lost a lot of blood and was only half conscious. The cortège swept past them and approached the swing doors of the Frontiersman. Con Meadows inside the saloon was urging his fellow outlaws to hold their fire. This mad escapade of the captain's had already cost him the windows of his new-found property. Here at least was a silver lining; maybe something could still be salvaged from the situation.

Upstairs by the window Parsons himself surveyed the scene triumphantly. Then something caught his eye. One of the two men at the rear of the group was pressing a handgun into Jack Hobb's back. Parsons shouted a warning to the two gunslingers downstairs – but too late.

As the warning rang out the cowboy, Pete Thompson, kicked the hapless Jack Hobbs viciously through the swing-doors and into the bar-room. Both Pete and the marshal caught sight of Fenton at the same moment and began throwing lead in his direction. He tried to fight back but, framed in the window, he was a sitting duck and two or three slugs brought him groaning to the floor.

Con Meadows had made his way to the staircase during the brief cease-fire. Now, hearing the shots and seeing Jack Hobbs hurtling towards him, gun in hand, his first thought was that Hobbs had betrayed them. He fired once and took half Jack's face away, then he retreated up the stairs exchanging shots with Pete Thompson's brother Max. Normally Con would have been more than a match for the young cowpoke, but now he was in a panic and firing wildly. Max took his time and fired once and got his reward as Meadows sagged backwards on to the stairs, eyes glazed over and his mouth wide open.

Paul Shand realized that somebody else was lurking in the shadows in the alleyway at the back of the saloon, but he had no way of telling if it was friend or foe. The new burst of firing seemed to be coming from inside the Frontiersman itself, but still Shand didn't dare stray from the recess where he was concealed.

Suddenly the door opened at the top of the outer staircase and Parsons appeared, closely followed by his henchman Mitch. They'd only descended a couple of steps when a shot rang out and a sliver of wood was torn from the handrail inches from Parsons' forearm. Parsons turned and fired into the shadows and a brief flurry of shots ensued between him and his hidden assailant. Shand heard a yelp in the alleyway that indicated that one of the bullets had hit home; at the same instant Parsons sank down on to the staircase clutching a shattered rib.

'Mitch,' he said through clenched teeth. 'Help me up.'

But Mitch was more concerned with his own safety. As Parsons clutched at his leg to detain him he roughly kicked his leader aside and continued down the steps. He hadn't even drawn his gun; he was hoping to walk calmly away from the carnage and get on the first horse he encountered in the back streets. Then he noticed Paul Shand standing in his path.

'You're under arrest, Mitch,' Shand informed him. 'This time you ain't getting away.'

The gunslinger surveyed the badge he was wearing with a mixture of amusement and contempt.

'OK, Mr Deputy Town Marshal,' he drawled. 'Take me in.'

Paul Shand's draw was smooth and fast, but even as he went through the motions he realized that it wasn't fast enough. The other outlaws hadn't exaggerated Mitch's prowess with a gun; every movement Shand made was a split second behind his opponent, and that split second could mean death. As Mitch's gun levelled a shot rang out. Mitch's jaw sagged as Parsons' slug smashed into his spine from behind. Shand fired, too, and mercifully his bullet penetrated the crippled gunfighter's heart and killed him instantly. And that wasn't the end of it: Shand kept firing at the crouched figure on the stairway until finally Parsons rolled sideways and landed with a dull thud on the hard clay below.

Only then did Paul Shand return his Colt to its holster. He'd killed the man who'd saved his life. And frankly, he didn't give a damn.

To make it easier for Nancy Field to care for them, Doc Gray installed both wounded men in the same room at the Evergreen boarding-house. Mantle lay on one bed with his thigh bandaged up, and the big cowboy Miles on the other with his shoulder strapped after taking a slug from Captain Parsons' .45. Neither injury was life-threatening, but the doc wouldn't release them till the danger of infection was over.

Mantle's first visitors were Paul Shand and Rose Talbot, who looked very happy to be together again. Shand had taken Alvin Powell to recover the hidden cache of money, and the lawman was going to contact the US Marshal to arrange the return of as much of it as possible to its rightful owners. As far as Powell was concerned, Shand and Mantle had wiped their slates clean by helping him clean up Larkwood.

Then came the two youngsters who'd saved Mantle's life. Jamie and Floyd had managed to preserve their modesty despite the adulation of the townsfolk. Mantle liked them. A day or two later Max and Pete Thompson called in to tell him the story he'd already been told by the big feller, in the other bed.

'When Dickens and his mob came into sight, we ran for cover,' Max admitted. 'We was scared stiff and cussing you for leaving us, Brad.'

'I ain't never been so scared,' his brother said. 'Jeff Dickens was breathing smoke through his nostrils and there was twelve of 'em backing him up. I guess it was the things he said to Sue Johns that changed our minds for us. He threatened to burn the whole place down, with her, the two kids and the *señora* inside. That's when we stopped thinking about our own skins. Miles grabbed his rifle and fired the first shot; then me and Max joined in.'

'I couldn't believe it when all them cowpokes turned tail at the first sign of trouble,' Miles chipped in from the other side of the room. 'Only Dickens and his hired guns stayed put to fight it out, and they was so far from cover we started bringing them down like a turkey-shoot. Jack Hobbs took no part in it; he jumped off his horse and hugged the ground till the rest of them was dead and we stopped firing. We brought him straight to town to hand him over to the marshal, but Powell had a better idea. I guess I already told you the rest,' he concluded, omitting his own brave contribution at the rear of the saloon.

Mantle sat up in the bed, looking very thoughtful.

'Who's looking after the ranch?' he asked suddenly. 'Who's tending the herd?'

'Stewart and Jones,' Pete Thompson replied. 'Sue reckoned they could cope for a few hours, just for us to pay you both a visit.'

'Sue reckoned . . .' Mantle exclaimed, his voice and his colour rising as he spoke. 'Who's the ranch foreman – Sue Johns or me? You left two men to do the work of six because Sue told you it was OK? The hell you did!'

Seated next door in the lounge of the guest-house Sue Johns and Nancy Field exchanged

glances as they sipped their tea. Both women
knew what the outburst meant: Brad Mantle was
on the mend.